MW00957843

CHOOSING SIDES

The Kids From
KENNEDY MIDDLE SCHOOL

CHOOSING SIDES

ILENE COOPER

MORROW JUNIOR BOOKS
NEW YORK

Copyright © 1990 by Ilene Cooper
All rights reserved.
No part of this book may be reproduced or utilized
in any form or by any means,
electronic or mechanical,
including photocopying, recording or by any
information storage and retrieval system,
without permission in writing from the Publisher.
Inquiries should be addressed to
William Morrow and Company, Inc.,
1350 Avenue of the Americas,
New York, NY 10019.

Printed in the United States of America.
5 6 7 8 9 10

Library of Congress Cataloging-in-Publication Data
Cooper, Ilene.
Choosing sides / Ilene Cooper.
p.   cm.—(The kids from Kennedy Middle School)
Summary: Jonathan doesn't want his father to think he's a quitter,
but middle school basketball—under the lash of a gung-ho coach—is
turning out to be anything but fun.
ISBN 0-688-07934-2
[1. Basketball—Fiction.   2. Choice—Fiction.   3. Schools—
Fiction.]   I. Title.   II. Series: Cooper, Ilene.
The kids from Kennedy Middle School
PZ7.C7856Ch   1990
[Fic]—dc20   89-13669   CIP   AC

For Bill,
a really good sport.
Thanks for all your help.

C H A P T E R
ONE

Jonathan Rossi was having trouble keeping his eyes on the ball. Even though this was just a pickup soccer game, Jonathan didn't want to let his teammates down. He tried to kick the ball away from the opposing players as they moved it toward the goal, but periodically Jonathan's gaze would shift to the sidelines, where Robin Miller and some of the other sixth-grade girls stood watching the game. At least they were supposed to be watching. At the moment, there was a lot of talking going on . . . and giggling. What was so funny? Jonathan wondered.

"Hey, heads up, Rossi!" Mike Stone called.

Jonathan snapped to attention, but it was

too late. He could only watch helplessly as the black-and-white soccer ball rolled right past him. Then a big foot appeared and kicked the ball back to the other side of the field.

"Way to go, Mike," Jonathan yelled, happy that someone was doing what he was supposed to.

"Should have been yours." Mike puffed as he ran past Jonathan, following the ball.

Stung, Jonathan was glad to hear the first bell clang. He was better off inside Kennedy Middle School if he was going to daydream the game away.

Walking off the field to the grass where most of the players had dumped their stuff, Jonathan picked up his sweater and Chicago Cubs cap, which he shoved on his head. Then he remembered how the cap mussed his hair, so he took it off and stuck it in his pocket. Running a hand through his straight dark hair, he hoped it was lying flat. Recently, he had noticed that when his hair wasn't combed properly, he looked a little like a porcupine.

"Hey, wait for me, Jon," a husky boy called from a few feet away, where he was trying to juggle several books, a lunch bag, and a pair of gym shoes.

"Well, then hurry up, Berger."

Out of the corner of his eye, Jonathan watched Robin and the other girls head toward the red brick building that some of the kids said looked more like a penitentiary than a school. Jonathan had only seen prisons in the movies, but Kennedy, the only middle school in Forest Glen, Illinois, sometimes felt like a jail, especially with Mrs. Volini, his teacher, striding up and down the aisle and monitoring her sixth graders' work. Mrs. Volini was nicknamed "Volcano" because she was always blowing her stack. Sometimes, the kids called her Mt. Volini.

A hand clapped down hard on Jonathan's shoulder. Jon didn't even have to look. Mike was the only one who used a death grip like that. "What is it, Stone?" Jonathan asked, shaking him off, though not very easily.

"Basketball tryouts."

"How could I forget? Coach Brown has been talking it up since school started."

Mike shrugged. "Just reminding you. If we're going to have a decent team, we need to start practicing." Before Jonathan could answer, Mike loped off toward the building. He was in the other sixth-grade class, taught by Mr. Jacobs, who marked people down for being late.

Mrs. Volini was even harder on latecomers. They sat on a bench outside the classroom until she called them back. That would have been all right if it meant missing math, but no one ever did. Mrs. Volini always made sure the tardy ones were called back in plenty of time for math.

Jonathan turned toward the tree where Kevin was now arguing with one of the fifth graders about whether the last goal of the soccer game counted. "Hey, Berger, let's go," Jonathan yelled.

Kevin made a final face at the kid and hurried toward Jonathan. Like Mrs. Volini, he had a nickname, too, even more inevitable— "Ham."

"Sorry," Ham said. "But I thought you were talking to Stone, anyway."

"He was just reminding me about basketball tryouts tomorrow."

Ham grinned, showing his chipped tooth. Even though his mother was insisting that he get it fixed, he didn't want to because he'd told everyone he had broken it in a touch-football game with some junior high kids. He had been playing that day, but the mishap didn't occur until later when he bit into some stale candy.

"Basketball's going to be great," he enthused. "It's about time we had a team."

"We had a team last year at the community center," Jonathan pointed out. He had been captain.

Ham kicked some crunchy dead leaves out of his way. "I mean an official team, one that can play other schools. It's just too bad we have to have those dorky fifth graders on it."

"They're not so bad," Jonathan said mildly. "Besides, without them, we might not have enough kids trying out."

"Yeah, usually there are three sixth-grade classes. Now they've stuffed everybody into two." Ham's round face broke into a smile. "But there is one good thing about having such big classes."

"What's that?"

"It makes you harder to find."

The hallway of Kennedy Middle School was filled with fourth, fifth, and sixth graders yelling, pushing, and slamming lockers before the second bell rang. Jonathan decided to keep his sweater with him and he strode into Mrs. Volini's room, almost bumping into Robin Miller.

"Hi, Jon," Robin said.

"Uh, hi." Jonathan turned and went to his seat. What was wrong with him, he wondered? He and Robin had had plenty of conversations since school started; they had even gone to The Hut for ice cream once. Lately, though, Jonathan got a funny feeling in his stomach when he got near Robin. It was the same sensation that he had before a test when he wasn't sure he had studied enough. He liked looking at Robin, and even thinking about her sometimes. Being right next to her was the problem.

As Jonathan got settled in his seat, he turned his attention to Mrs. Volini, who was writing something on the board. He squinted, trying to make out the words. Mrs. Volini wasn't very good at cursive writing. As far as he could tell, her phrase read, Amor Al Dil Emma. Who were Al and Emma?

When everyone was seated and the bell's last note had faded away, Mrs. Volini turned toward the class.

"Class, while I'm taking attendance, I want you to think about what I've written."

Think about it? Jonathan couldn't even decipher it. Several of the other kids looked bewildered, as well.

"Mrs. Volini?" Veronica Volner's voice was silky.

"Yes, Veronica?"

"It might be hard for some of the people at the back to read what you've written."

"That's very thoughtful of you, Veronica."

Jonathan picked at a nail. Oh right, he thought, like she would have mentioned it if she could have read it herself. Trust Veronica to make herself look good in Mrs. Volini's eyes.

"It says, A Moral Dilemma. Think about it while I take attendance."

Jonathan thought. Dilemma: That meant some kind of a problem. Moral was a little harder. The longer he stared at the word *moral*, the less familiar it looked. Maybe it meant more, more of a problem.

When Mrs. Volini finished checking off the last name, she turned her attention back to the class. "Well?" she asked.

All hands were down.

"You've never heard the phrase before?"

Heads were shaking all over the room.

Mrs. Volini sighed. "Then let me explain. A dilemma is a problem."

Jonathan sat up a little straighter. At least he was on the right track.

"And morality is a matter of right and wrong. I'll give you an example. You find a wallet with a hundred dollars in it. The owner's address is in the wallet, too. What do you do?"

"Return it." "Give it back." The class seemed in agreement about the proper course of action.

Mrs. Volini nodded. "That would be the honest thing to do. Now let me add something to the story. You are very poor. Say there's not enough money to feed your family. Do you still return it?"

Gretchen Hubbard raised her hand. "You might get a reward if you gave it back," she said hopefully.

"You might. But you might not. Robin?"

"Returning the money is right, so you have to do it."

"That's what you say now," Ham argued. "But if your family was really starving, I bet you'd keep it."

Mrs. Volini raised her voice over the several others that began speaking. "As you can see, this example I've given you raises a few questions. Now let me give you another one. A friend shoplifts; do you tell on him or her?"

The room quieted down considerably. Almost everyone knew somebody who had stolen something at one time or another.

"What if they ask you to take something out of the store for them? Do you participate?" Mrs. Volini waved away the comments. "Not now. We will have lots of time for discussion as we study a new unit entitled 'Truth or Consequences.'"

"I've got the home version," Ham called.

Mt. Volini looked as if she were starting to erupt. "Ham, we are not talking about a television show. I should have thought you would realize that from the conversation we've been having."

Ham began studying the top of his desk. "Sorry."

Pushing a loose hair over her ear, Mrs. Volini ignored Ham's apology and went on. "Until Christmas vacation, we will be talking about why people lie or cheat, and if it is ever justified. Governments do it sometimes, and some would say that advertisers stretch the truth. We will discuss those kinds of questions, and we will also talk about what is the right and wrong thing to do in certain everyday situations. Your final project, due after vacation, will be to write a composition about a moral dilemma. It can be one you've experienced or one you've heard about. Since I'd like you to do an especially good job on this, spend some time thinking before you write. Then, after the papers are handed in, we can talk about some of the dilemmas you've written about."

"Will you read them out loud?" Candy Dahl asked suspiciously.

"Not if you don't want me to. Just let me know and I will keep your composition confidential."

Jonathan stared at the science posters that decorated the room. What kind of moral dilemma was he going to write about? Oh well, he consoled himself, he had plenty of time to come up with one.

Right now, he had something more important on his mind. While he was supposed to be doing story problems, locating Australia on the map in his geography book, even when he was supposed to be singing (with zest, as his music teacher implored), Jonathan was picturing himself on the basketball court, slam dunking a ball to the cheers of his many fans.

Basketball was going to be his sport, he just knew it. Ham was right; their team at the community center really didn't count. It was just a bunch of boys goofing around, throwing baskets and missing most of them. Even so, the ball had felt good in his hands. The best part, though, was that he was tall and getting taller every minute.

It was important for Jonathan to find a sport that he was good at, because sports were very big in the Rossi house. Mr. Rossi watched every game that he could find: football, baseball, basketball, hockey—professional or college. He even watched sports Jonathan had barely heard of, like lacrosse.

Jonathan had already tried Little League baseball, but that definitely wasn't his sport. Swinging and hitting a ball or catching it with one hand seemed so easy when professional baseball players did it. Jonathan knew from personal experience that it was plenty hard. He had been secretly pleased when the park district had decided to end their Little League program. It was something about insurance that Jonathan didn't really understand, but his father had ranted and raved. Mr. Rossi had even missed a Bears football game on "Monday Night Football" to go to a city council meeting to protest their decision. When his father got home, muttering that the council members were un-American, Jonathan knew that he would be safe next summer.

*   *   *

Gym was the last class of the day and as the kids were filing out after a game of medicine ball, Coach Brown reminded Jonathan once more about basketball tryouts the next day. "We'll be looking for you tomorrow," the coach said as Jonathan stooped to tie his gym shoe. "You keep growing like that, and you're going to be another Larry Bird."

Jonathan knotted the bow smartly and stood up. "I'm going to go home and practice right after school, Coach."

But later, when he was closing his locker, Jonathan was waylaid by Robin Miller.

Jonathan stood up a little straighter. "Oh, hi, Robin."

"Jon, I . . . uh, I'm not taking the bus home today." Her faced turned red, almost the color of her curls.

"You're not?" Brilliant, Rossi, he immediately thought to himself. She just said she wasn't.

Robin didn't seem to notice his dumb remark. That was one thing Jonathan liked about her—she never acted as if he'd put his foot in it.

"No, I have to go to the library. And I was wondering, since that's the way you walk, if, uh, I could walk with you."

"Oh. Sure," Jonathan replied, hoping that he sounded casual yet cool.

Jonathan was planning to drop Robin off at the library and get home before it got too dark to shoot a few baskets, but it didn't work out that way. The Forest Glen Library was on the far edge of the suburb's small downtown. So, first, they stopped at the bakery and bought some doughnuts. Then they went into the drugstore and looked at the comic books. All the nervousness Jonathan had felt earlier in the day about being with Robin seemed to fade the more they talked together.

"Gee," Robin said, glancing at her watch, "I've got to get to the library or my mom will be picking me up before I've had a chance to do my history homework."

"Yeah. And I've got to go home and practice for basketball tryouts." Looking at the sinking sun, though, Jonathan realized he'd barely be able to see the hoop by the time he made it home.

"I'm sure you'll make the team," Robin said as they walked toward the impressive stone library building.

Jonathan tried to look modest. "Yeah, it should go okay."

On the way home, he thought about the

different kinds of athletic shoes he might buy.

"Hi, Mom," he said, bursting into the warm kitchen filled with enticing smells. His mother liked cooking, so the Rossi kitchen was pretty fancy. Copper pots and pans, gleaming in the light, hung from a big rack that was suspended from the ceiling. Jonathan jumped, as if he was making a free throw, and clanged two of them together.

Mrs. Rossi turned away from the stove. Her pleasant face, so much like Jonathan's, was pink from standing over a steaming pot of stew. "Oh, Jon, I hate when you do that," she said, but she smiled at him, anyway. "How was your day?"

"Great," Jonathan said, trying to sneak some cookies from the jar on the counter. Mrs. Rossi shook her head. "Not before supper." Then she glanced at the clock. "You're home late, aren't you?"

One nice thing about his mother: As long as her sons made it home before dinner was actually on the table, she never worried much about where they were.

"I stopped downtown," Jonathan said.

Mrs. Rossi wiped her hands on her apron. "You and Ham?"

"Uh, no," Jonathan replied, in what he hoped was a nonchalant voice. "Robin Miller."

He was glad to see his mother wasn't even trying to hide a smile. "That's nice," she said absently as she opened the cabinet and picked up one of the bottles of spices.

"Hey, Mom, when's dinner?" Jonathan's older brother, David, stomped into the kitchen and threw his books down on the counter.

"Soon."

"I have to be out of here by seven. Football practice," he said importantly.

"We know, David," Mrs. Rossi said patiently. "We're used to your schedule by now."

Ever since David had made the frosh-soph team at Forest Glen High, he had acted as if the world revolved around his football schedule. David's status as the quarterback irked Jonathan, but he had to admit it made him a little proud, too—not that he'd ever tell that to David.

"How about one of you guys setting the table?"

"I've gotta study, Mom," David protested.

"We're eating in"—she glanced at the clock—"fifteen minutes."

"I'll do it," Jonathan said with a sigh.

"Good boy." His mother beamed.

"Good boy," David repeated in a silly, squeaky voice. He bounded away from the counter, grabbed Jonathan, ruffled his hair, and then rubbed his knuckles into Jon's scalp. "Mama's little helper."

"Better than listening to you try and weasel out of it," Jonathan muttered as he twisted away.

"Hey . . . I said I've—"

"Boys, please," Mrs. Rossi said, raising her voice. "David, get to it. Now you've only got fourteen minutes."

"He can't even read a sentence in fourteen minutes," Jonathan said under his breath.

David was bulky but quick. Nevertheless, Jonathan sidestepped the leg David put out to trip him, grabbed some spoons, knives, and forks from the silverware drawer, and headed into the dining room. He'd come back for the dishes and glasses when it was safer.

Jonathan didn't know too many families that ate their meals in the dining room, but his father liked it. Oh, once in a while on Sunday, he'd consent to brunch in the kitchen, or he'd allow pizza in front of the television in the family room when an important game was on television. Those were the exceptions, however. Mr. Rossi enjoyed having his family gathered around him at the highly polished wood table, eating their supper, discussing the day's events.

Jonathan heard the front door open and the "clack" as his father dropped his keys on the hall table, but even without those audible cues, he would have known his father was home. Even as a little kid, Jonathan could feel the difference when his father stepped into the house. It was as if someone had turned up the volume.

"Home," Mr. Rossi said as he walked into the kitchen from the hall. "Where are the boys?" he asked, giving his wife a kiss on the cheek.

"David's upstairs studying until we eat. Which will be just as soon as you wash up."

"Good, I'm hungry. And Jon?"

"Here I am," Jonathan said, coming into the kitchen.

Mr. Rossi turned his gaze on his son. "Hey, kiddo, did you practice after school?"

Jonathan began taking dishes out of the cabinet next to the sink. "Uh, not exactly."

When Jonathan was little, he had always been fascinated by the way his father's bushy eyebrows met when he frowned. Jonathan had even spent time in front of the bathroom mirror trying to make his own, skinny eyebrows do the same thing, but he never could. Even then, though, he never liked those frowning eyebrows directed at him. The way they were now.

"What does 'not exactly' mean?" Mr. Rossi asked.

"I was busy after school, but I practiced in gym." It wasn't a lie. He had dribbled a little before class actually started.

"Mitch, he doesn't have to be playing basketball every minute," Mrs. Rossi said as she ladled stew into a tureen.

"He loves it," Mr. Rossi protested.

"I'm going to make the team," Jonathan put in as he slammed the cabinet door.

His father smiled. The eyebrows were now at their proper distance. "Of course you are." He ruffled Jonathan's hair, as David had, but his touch was gentle. "Now go get your brother."

Jonathan hurried into the dining room and put a dish at each place. "I forgot the napkins, Mom," he yelled as he dashed up the short set of steps to David's bedroom.

Going inside his brother's room was like

walking into a Chicago Bears souvenir shop. A blue-and-gold Bears T-shirt lay crumpled on the floor, and a pennant was stuck up over the desk. Posters were taped haphazardly on the walls, and from the ceiling, the greatest of them all, Number 34, Walter Payton, smiled down on David's bed.

David was not using the few minutes before supper to do his homework. Instead, he sat at his desk, studying his football playbook.

"Hey, food," Jonathan called from the doorway.

"All right, in a minute," David said, not looking up.

"Did the coach add some new plays?" Jonathan went into the room and peered over his brother's shoulder.

"A couple."

"You've only got a few more games. Why is he giving you new plays so late in the season?"

The sick expression on David's face made Jonathan wish he could make the words disappear. The coach was adding new plays because David wasn't doing very well calling the old ones. The team's two and four record was the proof of that.

Jonathan cast around in his mind for something to say that would make David feel better. "Maybe Dad got tickets for the Bulls game on Friday. He said he might."

David brightened. "That's right. Let's go see." He shoved his playbook in the desk drawer and slammed it shut.

By the time the boys got downstairs, Mr. Rossi was already seated at the table. His wife was putting out the napkins that Jonathan had forgotten—and the glasses.

"Dad, did you get Bulls tickets?" Jonathan asked as he slid into his seat.

Mr. Rossi tried to look somber, but a smile played around his lips. "Looks good."

"All right!" David whooped.

"I think I'll be able to get some seats for Thanksgiving weekend, too."

"Well, don't forget to get an extra one," Mrs. Rossi said, carefully laying her napkin on her lap.

"An extra one? You don't want to go, do you?"

"No, Mitch," Mrs. Rossi said patiently. "For Mark. Don't you remember? He and Janice will be here over Thanksgiving."

"Mark, that wimp . . ." David began.

"I don't want to hear it," Mrs. Rossi warned.

Jonathan ignored the fracas and spooned

into his stew. Their cousin Mark, Aunt Janice's son, was just between Jonathan and David in age and wasn't like them at all. He never used bad language, didn't much care about sports, and would rather be practicing the violin than throwing a ball any day of the week. Mr. Rossi always said Mark's problems stemmed from his father running off to be in the rodeo when Mark was only a baby.

"Anne," Mr. Rossi began in a reasonable tone, "it's hard to get Bulls tickets. Mark would probably prefer seats for the Chicago Symphony, anyway."

Mrs. Rossi gave her husband a steely glance.

"Look," he began again, "it's not my fault the kid's father decided he'd rather—"

"Rather rope calves than change diapers," Jonathan and David said in unison. Mr. Rossi had been saying that about Mark's dad for as long as they could remember.

"He's out of diapers, Mitch, and it would be nice if you showed some fatherly interest in him."

Mr. Rossi looked a little embarrassed. "I guess you're right. It's just that Mark's so different from our boys."

"Well, differences are what make life interesting," she said philosophically. "Janice and I aren't anything alike, but we have fun together. Always did."

Jonathan looked at his mother and tried to picture her as a young girl. It wasn't that difficult. With her hair pulled back in a ponytail, she still looked kind of young, especially when she smiled.

Mr. Rossi grinned at his wife. "You and I are awfully different."

"Yep. I don't care if the Bears go to the Super Bowl."

There were some good-natured catcalls from the male Rossis.

Mrs. Rossi laughed and held up her hands. "All right, I care. A little."

"You cared about football when I was the captain of the Illini," Mr. Rossi said, naming his college team at the University of Illinois.

"It's true," Mrs. Rossi admitted. "But I mostly cared about you. Your father was a big man on campus," she said to David and Jonathan.

"Oh, I wasn't that . . . exactly."

"Stop fishing for compliments, Mitch. You know you were."

"I guess people do look up to sports heroes," Mr. Rossi said. He turned his attention to his sons. "Did I ever tell you boys about the game I played against Michigan?"

He had, about a million times, but Jonathan didn't mind. He could listen to his father's stories and think about other things at the same time.

CHAPTER
TWO

Jonathan stood with the other boys in a semi-circle, waiting for his turn to shoot. So far during tryouts, each boy had taken five free throws and then had joined the others clustered around the lane, fighting for rebounds. Actually, there were plenty of rebounds for everyone, since few of the boys ever made a shot. The more Jonathan saw of the competition, the more he liked his chances. The fifth graders were completely hopeless. Only one of them had even managed to hit the rim with a shot. Jonathan knew that the Chicago Bulls announcer called a missed shot an airball. That hardly ever happened at a Bulls game, but here the airballs filled the gym like fireworks on the Fourth of July.

Coach Brown blew on his whistle after everyone had had a turn. "All right. Let's get a game going here." He barked out the names of five boys. "Shirts," he said. Then he picked out five more. "Skins."

Jonathan threw his shirt into the corner in disgust. It was too cold in this gym to be a Skin. A Shirt named Danny Wolfe bounded past him. "Nice goose pimples, Rossi." He laughed.

"Better than the pimples on your face," Jonathan shot back, but he envied the fleecy sweat shirt Danny had on.

With the coach's whistle, the game went into high gear. Dribble, pass, shoot. At least that's the way it was supposed to be, but none of the boys could consistently do any of the three. Jonathan, the tallest boy on his team, played center and was able to make a few points for the Skins. He wasn't happy with the way the ball rolled out of his hands several times, but the Skins were ahead, and that was the important thing.

"All right," Coach Brown yelled. "You guys to the sidelines. Let's get some other people in there."

As the coach began picking out a few other hopefuls, Jonathan found his shirt and slipped it over his head. Then he sat down to watch the rest of the tryouts. It was kind of painful.

Ham, coming off the court after his playing time, joined Jonathan. "We're in," he said confidently.

Ham was one of the guys who was only mediocre, but Jonathan didn't want to disillusion his best friend, so he just said, "Yeah, I think so."

Ham used the edge of his shirt to wipe his red sweaty face. "Hey," he asked, "have you heard anything about this dance?"

"What dance?"

"I dunno. Before I got here, all the girls were standing around the water fountain talking about some dance."

Jonathan shrugged. "Nobody said anything to me about it."

"It's probably just some girl plot."

"Girl plot?" Jonathan laughed. "What are you talking about?"

Ham stuck his legs out in front of him and picked at a scab on his knee. "You know. First it's going to be dances. Then it'll be dating." His lips pursed as if he was eating a pickle.

"You should like that. You're the one who's always talking about girls."

"Me?" Ham looked at him in astonishment.

Jonathan leaned against the wall. Well, it wasn't actually girls Ham talked about. It was more like sex. He glanced sideways at his friend. Ham didn't seem to get the connection. Before Jonathan could explain it to him, Coach Brown, his belly quivering a little, strode to the middle of the gym.

"All right, that's it for the tryouts. By the way, I've chosen a name for the team. Since the high school team is the Tigers, I thought we would be the Wildcats. How does that sound?"

There were cheers and some clapping. "When do we find out who made the team?" someone called.

"I'll be posting the players in the next day or so." He gave the boys an encouraging smile. "Now, hit the showers."

Jonathan would have liked just to have gotten dressed and gone home, but lately his mother was always telling him he smelled. When he'd asked her once what exactly he smelled like, she'd said, "Boy." Jonathan didn't see what was so wrong with that, but then she had gone into a long spiel about hormones, hygiene, and growing up. To avoid her getting on even more embarrassing subjects, Jonathan had gone upstairs for a shower that day. He supposed he'd take one now. The only thing he wanted to smell like when he got home was soap. It was one thing to hear about sex from Ham. It would be another to hear about it from his own mother.

Coach Brown was busy writing something on his clipboard. Jonathan willed him to turn around. He wanted confirmation that he had done a good job, but the coach just kept scribbling away. Slowly, Jonathan walked into the locker room.

Most of the boys were already in the large open shower area, the water beating down on them. There was a lot of hollering and laughing going on, but Jonathan grabbed a towel, stripped quickly, and turned on a shower head, keeping slightly away from the crowd. Making jokes about being naked in the shower was the rule rather than the exception, but Jonathan kept his mouth shut and his eyes averted.

He had just finished soaping up when Ham, who hadn't bothered with a shower, bounded into the locker room, his eyes wide.

"The coach fell down."

Mike Stone stuck out his head and said casually, "Well, pick him up."

"I'm not kidding," Ham insisted. "We were walking in the hall and he just slipped. His leg looked all twisted."

Now the boys scrambled out of the showers. Jonathan turned quickly under the pelting water and shut off the handles with a thud.

"Did you get help?" someone asked.

"I didn't have to. He banged against a locker when he fell and Mrs. Reiter came out of her room to see what made the noise. She ran down to Mr. Thomas's office."

Jonathan pulled his T-shirt over his head. "Then what?" he demanded.

Ham sat down on a bench. "It was horrible. I had to talk to him. I mean, I had to say things, like, 'Don't worry, Coach, it'll be all right.' "

There were a few nervous snickers.

Ham scowled. "Listen, it wasn't easy staying out there while he moaned."

"He was moaning?" Mike asked as he tied his shoes.

Ham let out what Jonathan supposed was a groan, but it sounded more like a cow mooing. Then he said, "There's an ambulance coming.

29

I waited until Mr. Thomas came and told the coach it was on the way. Then I came here."

"What are we waiting for?" Jonathan asked. "Let's get going."

The herd of basketball players stumbled toward the hall. Down the corridor, two white-uniformed paramedics were gently lifting the coach—who was still clutching his leg—onto a stretcher. The boys ran to get a closer look, but Mrs. Reiter motioned them back, away from the activity.

The boys had been talking nervously among themselves, but seeing the coach, his face creased with pain, quieted them down. They watched silently as he was covered with a blanket and carried out the double doors, with the principal, Mr. Thomas, and several teachers right behind him.

With Mike in the lead, the boys moved outside and watched one of the attendants slam the door. With a squeal of brakes and a scream of the siren, the ambulance pulled away.

When it was out of sight, Jonathan hesitantly went up to Mr. Thomas. "How is he?" he asked.

Mr. Thomas was always an imposing figure, even when he was smiling. Now his expression was somber. "They think his leg is badly fractured." He turned to Ham. "You were with him, right, Berger? What happened?"

Ham shrugged helplessly. "We were walking along and he slipped."

"I saw gum on the bottom of Coach Brown's shoe," Mrs. Reiter said, her face grim.

Jonathan noticed that one or two of the boys who were chewing gum quickly swallowed.

"Carelessness," Mr. Thomas muttered. "An accident that didn't have to happen." He caught sight of the basketball players huddled together. "I think it's time you boys went home."

There seemed no reason to stay, so they wandered back to the locker room to get their coats and books.

A short fifth grader who hadn't gotten the ball through the hoop once asked, "Are we still going to have a team?"

"You're not going to be on it, if we are," Mike said, giving his gym locker a slam.

The boy looked down at his shoes.

"Hey, Stone, lay off," Jonathan said.

"Truth is truth."

"But we do have to have a team soon," Ham said worriedly. "The schedule's already been printed."

Paul Marks, a skinny kid with thick glasses,

whose large hands could be good for passing a basketball, glared at the others. "What about the coach? He's more important than some stupid schedule."

"Aw, he'll be all right," Ham replied, but he looked embarrassed.

Jonathan shoved a few books in his backpack. "We ought to send him a card or something."

Ham brightened. "That's a good idea."

"You get one, Rossi," Mike said.

"Why me?" Jonathan protested.

"You're the guy who loves reading so much. You'll find something real poetic."

Mike had a way of pushing Jonathan's buttons. "All right, I will get one," he said defiantly.

"Fine," Mike said. "Sign my name."

"Maybe I will, maybe I won't." He flipped a finger at Stone and walked out the door.

Jonathan looked at his watch. There was still time to go over to the drugstore and pick out a card from their small, manageable selection. He might as well do it now.

But picking out the right kind of card wasn't as easy as Jonathan thought it would be. He spun the wire holder around, reading almost every get-well card. None of them seemed quite right. Either they were really sappy—"Our thoughts are with you during your illness"—or they were supposed to be funny but missed. "Hope you'll soon be feeling in the pink" read a card that showed a patient standing in a field of pink flowers. All the rest featured needles, or thermometers, or—yuk—bedpans.

He reached up and pulled down one featuring a blond nurse on the cover. "Feeling bad?" it read. Jonathan flipped it open. "Ask the nurse if she can make it all better."

Somehow, Jonathan couldn't quite see the coach chuckling as he read that. He placed it back on the rack. Now what?

"Who's sick?"

Jonathan turned and looked down at Bobby Glickman. If Jonathan was one of the tallest kids in the sixth grade, Bobby had to be one of the shortest. He and Bobby never really hung out together, mostly because Bobby wasn't into sports. But he had his own claim to fame. He went to acting classes at the Beech Street Theater and had been in a couple of television commercials.

"Coach Brown fell and hurt his leg," Jonathan informed him.

"Is it broken?"

Jonathan nodded. "Mr. Thomas said it was. It was twisted in a real weird position. I was elected to get him a card."

Bobby glanced at the card rack. "They have lousy cards here."

"I've noticed."

"Why don't you go to the Card Barn? Some of their cards are funny. Funnier, anyway."

"Good idea," Jonathan said. He hesitated for a moment, wondering whether he should ask Bobby to go with him. Normally, he wouldn't, but he really didn't feel like making this decision alone. Besides, Bobby was always wising off in class. He should be able to spot a funny card.

"Want to come with me?"

Bobby shrugged. "Sure."

The wind was whipping off Lake Michigan, and Jonathan had to clutch the collar of his jacket closed to keep warm. The boys didn't say much until they crossed the street and entered the brightly lighted Card Barn. Jonathan looked around helplessly. The place was wall-to-wall cards. He didn't know where to begin.

Bobby had already left his side and was walking confidently up to the saleslady. "Get-well cards, please."

She pointed to the far wall. "They're over there. Let me know if I can help."

"Thanks," Bobby said, wearing his television smile. "We sure will."

Jonathan marveled. He hated to ask for help in a store and would wander around, lost, before he'd do it. Still, walking over to the huge get-well section, he could see that asking had its advantages. It certainly saved time.

Before Jonathan even had a chance to pick up a card, Bobby seemed to have scanned the section. "Look, here's one," he said, plucking it out of its holder.

On the cover was a man with a broken leg in a huge cast. It read, "You have a broken leg"; and on the inside, "And we're broken up about it."

Jonathan smiled. "Perfect."

Bobby studied the card. "This guy even looks like the coach."

That wasn't exactly a compliment. The man was bald, with only a fringe of hair ringing his head, and had a potbelly, but Bobby was right. There was more than a passing resemblance to Coach Brown.

"Maybe he'll take offense," Jonathan worried.

"Nah, he's not the type. Let's pay for it."

There was an awkward moment after the boys stepped outside. "Do you want to come over to my house for a while?" Bobby finally asked.

Jonathan had never been to Bobby's house before. Then he figured, Why not? He still had a little time before dinner. "Sure," he said. "I'll just call my mom when we get there."

It was a short walk to Bobby's house. Although the boys didn't live that far from each other, Bobby's house was just a block from the lake, in the ritziest part of town. Jonathan's house was a nice but ordinary split-level; Bobby's was reminiscent of a castle. It was set back on a wide expanse of lawn, and the house's most noticeable feature was its two round turrets.

"Hey do those things mean some of the rooms are round?" Jonathan asked as they climbed the stone stairs.

"Yeah. One of them's mine."

Jonathan called his mother, and then the boys got some cookies and milk and headed up to Bobby's room. Jonathan stood gaping in the doorway. This had to be the most interesting room he had ever seen.

Not only was it circular but the effect was

heightened by wraparound laminate furniture that was built into the walls. Even the bunk beds had a slight curve to them. From the ceiling hung several airplanes, much larger than the models that were built from kits.

"Great," he exclaimed.

"Yeah, it's okay."

"Okay?"

"Well, my mom picked out most of the stuff," Bobby said with embarrassment. "I don't even like airplanes."

"Hey, what's that?" Jonathan asked, noticing a ladder that seemed to be attached to the wall.

"Oh, this is kind of cool." Bobby jumped on the ladder and, using the bottom rung as a scooter, coasted around the room. "See, it's on a track," Bobby said, pointing to a metal attachment that circled the room and stopped at the bunk beds. "It's for climbing to the top bunk."

"Can I try it?" Jonathan asked eagerly.

Bobby stepped off. "Go ahead."

Jonathan went back and forth from the bed to the window a couple of times before he started to feel dumb. Still, it was a fun thing to have in your room.

"Let's see, what else can I show you?" Bobby asked, a little nervously. Jonathan wondered how often Bobby had kids over.

"What about stuff from your commercials?"

"I have them all on videotape. But I don't really have any souvenirs or anything."

"Robin got a NO DRUGS T-shirt when she was in that TV spot."

Robin attended acting classes at the Beech Street Theater with Bobby and had recently lucked into a public-service announcement. She hadn't been picked because of her talent but, rather, for her red hair, which was almost the same color as that of the carrot-topped rock star who appeared in the spot with her.

Bobby flopped down on the lower bunk. "Yeah. Well, I got a free case of cornflakes once, but I don't think you want to see that."

Jonathan laughed. "Guess not." He looked around the room. Bobby had a lot of books on his shelf. There was a mystery Jonathan had been meaning to read for a while but had never gotten around to. "Hey," he asked, going over and picking it up, "can I borrow this?"

"Sure. Say, you like to read, right?"

Jonathan nodded as he flipped through the pages of the book.

"Why don't you try out for Battle of the Books?"

Battle of the Books was neat. The school librarian, Miss Morris, handed out a list of books to the sixth graders. Any three kids could form a team, and then they battled off against other teams, answering questions about the books they had read. The Kennedy winner played winners from other schools.

Jonathan looked up with interest. "That might be fun."

"You get to read a lot of good stuff." Bobby looked at him shrewdly. "And Robin said she wanted to be on a team."

"Oh, yeah?" Jonathan kept his tone non-committal. "Well, I might do it."

"So, are you going to the dance with Robin?"

Jonathan dragged the comfortable-looking denim chair from the corner and pulled it next to the bed. "What about this dance? Ham mentioned it, too."

"It's at the community center, the Saturday after we get out for Christmas vacation. It's for sixth, seventh, and eighth graders."

"Dates?"

"I guess anybody can go, but from what the girls are saying, they want to go with dates."

Jonathan stared up at the ceiling. This would be a first. Even though he and Robin spent time together, he wouldn't exactly call those excursions dates. For one thing, they had been during the day. This definitely sounded like a nighttime affair.

"I guess I'll go with Robin," he said slowly. "What about you?"

Bobby shrugged. "I don't know."

"Plenty of girls would like to go with you, I'll bet."

"Just because I've been on television."

"No," Jonathan protested, though it was true that the kids, both boys and girls, treated Bobby differently because of his acting.

"Well, I'll probably find someone."

The boys were silent for a minute.

"Hey, Jon, do you feel kind of weird about going to a real dance?"

It wasn't something Jonathan would have said, but he had to admit that Bobby was right.

"I mean a party is one thing," Bobby continued, "but this is different."

Jonathan ran a hand through his brown hair. "Bobby, what are we getting ourselves into?"

Bobby sighed. "I think my mother calls it puberty."

"Oh, puberty." It was the same reason that his mother had given him for having that "boy" smell. Jonathan gazed out the window and thought about puberty. Anything that caused body odor and made people start going to dances couldn't be good. Of that, Jonathan was sure.

C H A P T E R

THREE

The lunchroom was at the height of its usual noisy activity. Jonathan was sitting with Ham and Mike and a few of the other guys who had tried out for the basketball team, discussing when the names of the team would be posted.

"I heard that Coach Brown sent a list in from the hospital," Ham said. His mouth was full of spaghetti, the lunchroom special.

"Who told you that?" Paul Marks demanded.

Ham looked a little guilty. "I overheard Mr. Thomas talking to some guy in the office."

"What guy?"

"I don't know." He shrugged. "But he was

big. He looked a little like Arnold Schwartzenegger with yellow hair."

"Terminator," Mike said, lifting his arms as though he held a rifle. He pointed the imaginary rifle at Jonathan.

Jonathan crumpled up his brown paper lunch bag, threw it over Mike's arms, and made a perfect shot into the large plastic garbage can that stood in the middle of the aisle.

"All right," Ham cheered.

"So when are they posting this list?" Mike demanded.

Ham shrugged. "I didn't hear that."

"Then how are we supposed to find out?" Danny Wolfe asked.

"Maybe we could ask Mr. Thomas," Jonathan said.

The other boys looked at him aghast. Mr. Thomas was hardly the type anyone would willingly engage in conversation.

Jonathan looked around the table. "Well, it's not that big a deal." Since he had brought it up, Jonathan felt he should stand by his idea.

"I wouldn't do it," Ham warned.

Paul Marks took off his glasses and played with the frames. "A couple of weeks ago, Mr. Thomas saw me coming in after the second bell and he gave me a day's detention."

"What about the time he made my mother come to school just because he said I was running in the hallway?" Ham reminded Jonathan. "And I was running to the bathroom," he added righteously.

"The guy's a dictator," Mike said flatly.

"We'll find out who made the team eventually," Danny said. "You don't have to ask him special."

Jonathan didn't say anything. Maybe going to talk to Mr. Thomas wasn't such a hot idea.

Mike looked at Jonathan slyly. "Of course, if you think you're such a big shot, go ahead and do it."

Jonathan hesitated. "Maybe I will."

"When?"

Jonathan knew he was backed into a corner, right where Mike wanted him to be. Finally, with all the boys looking at him, he said, "After school. I'll stop in the office after school."

Mike smiled. "Good. I'll wait outside to see what happens."

Ham and Paul looked at each other.

"I guess we'll come, too," Paul said slowly, and Ham nodded.

"Okay." Jonathan stood up and started gathering his books. "No problem." But he was mentally kicking himself for shooting off his big mouth.

Jonathan glanced at the clock and then over at the lunch table where Robin was sitting with her friends Sharon and Gretchen. As if she could feel his glance, Robin looked up, and then quickly turned away.

It wasn't the first time today that they had caught each other's eye. Everybody knew about the dance by now and Robin was probably wondering why he hadn't asked her yet.

Jonathan wasn't sure himself. Mike Stone had already asked Candy Dahl. Ham kept saying there were several girls on his list, not that he had done anything about winnowing it down yet.

One of Jonathan's problems was that he couldn't quite figure out how to do the actual asking. Even having a chat with Mr. Thomas seemed easier than choking out the words *Robin, do you want to go to the dance at the community center?* Maybe he could just write her a note.

When three o'clock came, Mike, Ham, and Paul huddled outside Mr. Thomas's office, waiting for him to make his move. Jonathan wished he could send a note to the principal, as well. He must have been nuts to have come up with this idea, but he wasn't about to let the guys know that.

He tried to put a swagger in his walk as he approached the trio. "So? Is he in there?"

"That's for you to find out." Mike smirked.

Jonathan glanced through the glass doors of the office. Mrs. Hildebrand, the fussy school secretary, was filing some papers in a cabinet. Behind her, Mr. Thomas's door was firmly shut.

"You know, they're probably going to post that notice outside the gym any minute," Ham said worriedly. "Or it might be there already. Maybe we should go check."

"I checked on my way down," Mike replied. "It isn't."

Paul pushed his slipping glasses up the bridge of his nose. "I'd like to make the second bus. I mean, I'll wait if you're going to do this. . . ."

"I am," Jonathan said, but he didn't move.

The boys looked at him expectantly.

"Okay, I'm going right now." Humming a little tune under his breath, he walked inside the office. Fully aware of his friends' eyes boring into his back, he waited until Mrs. Hildebrand looked up from her filing.

"Yes?" she said with a frown.

"I'd like to see Mr. Thomas."

"Do you have an appointment?" she asked in a tone that indicated she knew he did not.

"No," Jonathan admitted.

"Mr. Thomas doesn't see students without an appointment. Usually, it is he who has made the appointment," Mrs. Hildebrand said pointedly.

Jonathan felt relief wash over him. It wasn't his fault Mr. Thomas wouldn't see him. Even that dork Stone should be able to understand that.

He was about to turn away when Mr. Thomas's heavy door flew open. The principal stood in the doorway, his eyes on Mrs. Hildebrand. Then they fell on Jonathan. "Rossi, are you being helped?"

Before Jonathan could answer, Mrs. Hildebrand said, "He was asking to see you."

Mr. Thomas raised his eyebrows. "What about?" he asked, directing his question to Jonathan.

Jonathan glanced over his shoulder at the guys. Then he cleared his throat. "I, uh, wanted to know if the names of the basketball team were going to be posted. The first game is next week."

"Come into my office, Rossi."

Jonathan didn't want to go. He had never actually been inside Mr. Thomas's office, and that was a record he wanted to keep intact. With Mr. Thomas frowning at him, though, Jonathan could see only one path open to him—through the door. Reluctantly, he followed Mr. Thomas inside.

Jonathan looked around curiously. It was a very tidy office. Mr. Thomas's desk was clean and the only thing on the wall was the principal's college degree, framed in black. He squinted his eyes, trying to read the name of the school Mr. Thomas had attended, but like Mrs. Volini's attempts at cursive writing, the fancy script was too hard to decipher.

"Here you are," Mr. Thomas said, thrusting a piece of paper at him. "Why don't you save Mrs. Hildebrand a trip and post this on the gym bulletin board."

"It's the list?"

"Yes, of course." He glanced at it. "I see your name is at the top."

"It is?" Jonathan asked excitedly.

Mr. Thomas smiled slightly. "It seems you are the new center."

Jonathan wanted to yell "All right," but he

restrained himself. Instead, he took the piece of paper and said, "Thanks, I'll put it up right now."

"Fine." Mr. Thomas had dismissed him.

Jonathan had another question. "How is the coach?"

"He is doing better. And he told me he received a card signed by some of you boys. It was much appreciated."

Jonathan reddened. "Oh, it was nothing."

"Unfortunately, he'll have to rest at home for several weeks at least. Then he may need some surgery."

"So who's going to coach?" Jonathan asked hesitantly.

"A substitute gym teacher has been hired. You'll be meeting Mr. Davidson during your practice session tomorrow. Don't forget to post that list now," Mr. Thomas said as he pulled a book off the shelf next to him.

Jonathan hurried back into the hallway, clutching the piece of paper. His friends gathered around him.

"You were in there so long," Ham said.

"But you look like you're in one piece," Mike added coolly.

Jonathan didn't want the boys to think it had

gone too easily. "You know Thomas. He gave me the third degree for a while. Demanded to know what I wanted."

Ham's eyes widened. "Did he yell or anything?"

"I wouldn't say yelled." Jonathan tried hard to look bored. "I just told him we were tired of being left in the dark about the basketball team. Then he gave me this." He wiggled the paper in front of them.

Mike grabbed it out of his hand. "It's the names of the team. I'm the forward," he whooped.

Ham peered over Mike's shoulder. "Guard," he said with satisfaction. "You, too, Paul."

Paul looked relieved. "I wasn't sure I'd make it at all."

"You're not too good," Mike said bluntly, "but you were better than any of the fifth graders."

Mike took the list back and scanned it. "Danny Wolfe is the other starting forward. And then there are a bunch of backups."

"What are you supposed to do with that list?" Ham asked.

"Put it up outside the gym. Oh, and there's

one other thing. We're going to have a new coach until Mr. Brown gets back."

"Who's that?" Mike demanded.

"A guy named Davidson."

"Boy," Mike said, "you and Thomas sure had yourself a chat." He poked Ham in the side. "Better watch out, Berger; looks like Rossi's got himself a new best friend."

Jonathan just gave him a superior smile and walked upstairs to post the list.

When Jonathan got home, there was no one around. He looked on the message board and found a note from his mother saying she'd be home from the library in time to start dinner.

Mrs. Rossi was taking courses to get her teaching certificate. His father would have preferred that she stay home and "just take care of her family," as he put it when she announced her intentions. But Mrs. Rossi had retorted, "My family is getting old enough to take care of themselves, especially you."

Jonathan took the stairs two at a time, intending to start his homework, but he heard music coming softly from David's room, and so he poked his head inside.

David was stretched out on his bed, studying his playbook. He had won his last game, but Jonathan had heard Mr. Rossi tell him not to rest on his laurels. Apparently, David was taking the advice seriously.

"Hey, Dave . . ."

David glanced up at Jonathan and then stuck his nose back in the book. Jonathan turned to leave, then came back inside.

"I'm busy, Jon," he said, shifting his bulk and turning a page.

"I know, but I wanted to tell you something. I made the basketball team. I'm the center."

"Good work." David gave him the thumbs-up sign before going back to his reading.

Jonathan waited until David noticed that he was still standing in the doorway. "I want to ask you something, too."

David threw his playbook aside and sat up. "Okay, I can see that I'm not going to get anything done here until I've taken care of you. What's happening?"

Jonathan cleared his throat. "There's going to be a dance at the community center."

"So?"

"I want to ask Robin," Jonathan mumbled.

"Yeah? What's stopping you?"

"I . . . I'm not sure how to do it."

"How about saying, Robin, want to go to the dance?"

Jonathan looked embarrassed. "I know what to say, but every time I see her, I walk in the other direction. It's like my mouth wants to do one thing and my feet do another."

"Nerves," David said with a knowing nod. "I've got the solution, buddy."

"You do?" Jonathan asked eagerly.

"Call her up and ask her."

Jonathan looked doubtful. "You mean it's easier on the telephone?"

"Sure it is. First of all, she can't see you, so if you do something dumb, like scratch yourself while you're talking, she'll never know."

"That's true." Jonathan nodded.

David warmed to his topic. "Maybe her mom will be standing right next to her, so she's not going to want to talk too much. And when you want to get off, just tell her I need to use the phone. That way, the conversation won't go on too long."

"David, you're a genius!"

David waved his hand. "Hey, I've been through it all myself. Why don't you call before Mom gets home."

"Good idea." Then Jonathan felt the familiar

butterflies starting to flap their wings in his stomach. "But it's still going to be hard to dial the number."

"I have a trick for that, too. Don't think about what you're doing while you dial. Keep your mind on something else. Make a list of the highest scorers in the NBA, or name the last five World Series champs. The next thing you know, she's answering and you're talking. It's an automatic response."

Jonathan felt cheered; then he had another thought. "But what do I do if her mother answers?"

David picked up the playbook and started reading. "Oh, that's easy. You hang up."

Jonathan decided it was now or never. He marched downstairs to the telephone in the kitchen, where he would have more privacy. There was no need to look up Robin's number. He had memorized it weeks ago.

"The Los Angeles Dodgers, 1988," he whispered as he dialed. The phone began ringing. "Boston Red Sox, 1987. New York—"

Robin's voice interrupted with a soft hello.

Clearing his throat, Jonathan said, "Hi, Robin, it's Jonathan."

"Oh, Jonathan."

There was a silence that went on too long for

Jonathan's comfort. Then they both started speaking at the same time. "I was calling . . ." "Did you want something . . ."

"Sorry," Robin said, just before Jonathan could get the word out.

He took a breath. "Well, I was just calling to see if you wanted to go to the community-center dance. With me, I mean."

"Sure, Jon, I'd like that."

Thinking it might be rude just to say good-bye after issuing his invitation, Jonathan was about to launch into the story of his bold meeting with Mr. Thomas, but before he could get started, Robin said regretfully, "I have to get off. My dad needs to use the phone."

"Oh. Okay. Well, I'll see you tomorrow."

"Jon . . ."

"Yes?"

"Thanks for calling."

"Sure. Bye." He put the phone back on its hook. Grabbing a cookie from the jar on the counter, he took a huge bite. Then, with a whoop, he took the stairs two at a time, headed for his room. Center of the basketball team and a date with Robin all in one day. All right!

C H A P T E R

FOUR

Big, blond, and dressed in crisp white shorts and a tight-fitting T-shirt, Coach Davidson resembled an iceberg, and Jonathan had already crashed into him once.

If only he hadn't gotten to the gym before any of the other guys. Then he would have been just one of the group. But Mrs. Volini had sent him to the office with a message, and since it was so close to the bell, she told him he didn't have to come back to class. So Jonathan left the message with Mrs. Hildebrand, changed his clothes in the locker room, and then wandered into the gym.

He grabbed a basketball from the wire container where they were kept and started dribbling. The rhythmic bounce of the ball was interrupted by a deep voice saying, "Who are you?"

Jonathan caught the ball and looked up with a smile. "I'm Jonathan Rossi. The new center."

Mr. Davidson looked down at him from an awesome height. There was no responding smile as he replied, "I'll be the judge of that."

Jonathan immediately felt the chili dog he had had at lunch do a swan dive in his stomach. "Coach Brown already picked the team," Jonathan tried to explain.

"We'll start with that team. Then we'll see."

"Oh."

"I suggest you keep practicing your dribbling." His tone indicated Jonathan could use the practice.

One by one, the rest of the team wandered in. When they were all assembled, Coach Davidson blew hard on his whistle. "Line up."

The boys meandered into something resembling a line. Coach Davidson looked at them with disdain. "The first thing you'd better learn is how to line up. Stand up straight! Get next to each other!"

The boys hurriedly arranged themselves. A few of them exchanged looks.

"That's better. I have been informed by one of you that he is the center of this basketball team."

All heads swiveled toward Jonathan, who examined a crack in the ceiling.

"I know that Coach Brown chose a team before his unfortunate accident. However, I am reserving the right to make some changes on that team after I assess your playing ability. Is that understood?"

Everyone nodded.

"We will begin by having a practice game." He barked out the names of Coach Brown's team and then of five other boys. "All right," he said, throwing the ball to Mike. "Let's play and see how you do."

They didn't do very well. None of the boys had really played together as a team. Some of the fifth graders could barely dribble and even the older boys had difficulty holding on to the ball when it was thrown to them. Hardly anyone made a basket. After ten minutes, Coach Davidson blew on his whistle and gestured for them to get into a circle.

"That was pathetic," he said bluntly.

Jonathan silently agreed with his assessment.

"We have a lot of work to do here."

One of the fifth graders raised his hand. "Yes?"

"Are we going to have uniforms?"

"Uniforms?" Mr. Davidson responded sarcastically. "I wouldn't worry about uniforms if I were you. You can't pass, you can't dribble, you can't throw. Uniforms should be the last of your concerns."

It was a dumb question, but Jonathan felt sorry for the kid who had asked it. The boy was standing with his arms folded tightly in front of him, trying to look invisible.

Coach Davidson glanced around the room and his eyes fell upon Ham. "Some of you are not even in decent physical condition. Well, we're going to fix that. We're going to do laps. We're going to do push-ups. And we're going to practice until you eat, sleep, and dream basketball. Is that understood?"

There were a few mumbled yeses.

"Yes, sir!" The coach instructed them.

"Yes, sir!" the boys replied in unison.

"Now drop and give me twenty."

Some of the boys got into the push-up position, but others stood there, bewildered.

"Twenty push-ups," Coach Davidson yelled. "You know how to do push-ups, don't you?"

Jonathan thought he did, but apparently they weren't the right kind of push-ups for Coach Davidson. He came over and adjusted Jonathan's elbows, and then he moved over to Mike and flattened his back. Poor Ham could only manage about eight push-ups before he sat up, huffing and puffing.

Jonathan was concerned about the coach's reaction to Ham's performance, but Davidson barely glanced at the red-faced Ham as he said, "Don't worry, you'll all be doing twenty push-ups by the time I'm done with you. And more."

After the push-ups, Coach Davidson demonstrated some of the finer points of passing the basketball, and then he had the boys practice, over and over again. It was boring, but by the time the coach blew his whistle, they were doing better.

"Plan on practicing every Monday, Wednesday, and Friday," the coach informed them.

Paul Marks bit his lip, and then called out. "I have piano lessons on Mondays."

"Piano lessons." The words hung there. Finally, one or two of the boys repeated "Piano lessons," and started giggling.

"I guess you're going to have to decide whether you'd rather be a pianist or a basketball player," Coach Davidson said. "Dismissed."

"Hey pee-inist." Mike laughed as he ran by Paul.

Paul followed him glumly, with Jonathan and Ham walking alongside. "My mom's going to have kittens when I tell her I have to miss my piano lesson," he said.

"Are you sure you want to?" Ham asked, wiping the sweat from his brow.

Paul shrugged. "I'm not going to quit the team."

Jonathan flipped his locker open. "Nobody's going to quit," he said firmly. "Davidson's tough, but let's face it, we weren't very good out there."

"We were lousy," Ham said honestly.

"So, maybe we need someone who's going to make us improve."

Mike wandered over on his way to the shower, a towel wrapped around his middle. "That Davidson guy better remember I'm the starting forward."

"He said nobody's position is secure," Jonathan reminded him.

"He didn't get a chance to really see me in action. No one is going to take that position away from me."

Jonathan wished he felt that confident. As the hot water pelted down on him, he went over the players in his mind, how each had handled the ball, what everyone looked like as they threw the ball into the net—or toward it, anyway.

Maybe I'm not so bad, Jonathan thought to himself. At least nobody seemed much better.

By dinnertime, he had himself convinced. "I'm one of the best players on the team," Jonathan said as he took a bite of his hamburger. On Tuesdays, Mrs. Rossi had a late class and David and Jonathan ate with their dad at The Hut, a shack with the best hot dogs and hamburgers in town.

"Well, I should hope you are," Mr. Rossi replied. "Pass the mustard, please."

"That Davidson is really going to be on our case, Dad. He said we're going to be eating and sleeping basketball."

"My coach said the same thing about football," David said. "He was right, too."

"Didn't you mind?" Jonathan asked. "I mean, ever since school started, you've been spending all your time on football."

"Jon," Mr. Rossi began mildly, "I thought you understood, from what I've told you about my playing days, and what you've seen David do, that you've got to expect to work hard."

"Oh, I do," Jonathan said, trying to recoup.

"Once you get discipline, you can take that with you into other sports," Mr. Rossi explained. "David's football season will be over after Christmas, but what he's learned about good work habits he can carry over to his baseball practice."

Without any emotion, David said, "I can do some of the same arm exercises for pitching that I used to practice quarterbacking."

Jonathan didn't say anything, but he knew that David wasn't nearly as interested in baseball as he was in football. He had even told Jonathan that he wished Little League had been canceled when he was younger. Yet here he was talking about baseball season as if it was something he was anticipating.

He should tell Dad he doesn't want to play baseball, Jonathan thought. Although as he watched his father happily assessing the chances of the Forest Glen baseball team, Jonathan could see why his brother didn't want to do that.

"Did you ever have any coaches you didn't like, Dad?" Jonathan asked curiously.

Mr. Rossi smiled slightly. "Oh sure. My college football coach and I didn't get along at first."

"How come?" David asked.

"He didn't like the fact that I wore an earring," Mr. Rossi said.

Jonathan and David exchanged horrified glances. Their father, the accountant, with an earring! It couldn't be.

Mr. Rossi took in the boys' reaction with an amused smile. "Most of the guys wore their hair long then, even the jocks. I, however, was the only one on the team who insisted on an earring."

Peering at his father's ear, Jonathan said, "I don't see a hole."

"It closes up if you don't put anything in it. I haven't worn an earring for a long time."

He certainly never had worn one in all the time Jonathan had known him.

"So what happened?" David demanded. "Did you get to keep wearing it?"

"No. I realized that playing and getting along with the coach was more important to me than some fool earring, so I took it off."

Suddenly, Jonathan had a thought. "Dad, was giving up the earring a moral dilemma?"

Mr. Rossi swiveled in his seat to look at

Jonathan. "A moral dilemma? What the heck do you know about moral dilemmas?"

"Not much," Jonathan admitted. "Not enough." He outlined his assignment from Mrs. Volini and finished by saying, "I really haven't come up with anything to write about."

"What an assignment!" Mr. Rossi snorted. "They should be teaching you kids to read and do fractions."

"Dad, we learned fractions in the fourth grade."

"I know that. I simply meant you should be learning practical things. Your teachers don't need to be filling your head with"—he searched for the word—"concepts."

Jonathan was offended. It was as if his father didn't believe he could think for himself.

"Well, I think the assignment is interesting," he said huffily. He hadn't up until now, but suddenly Jonathan felt compelled to defend it.

As the practice sessions went on, the only dilemma on an exhausted Jonathan's mind was how to keep up with his homework and basketball practice.

Each session was the same. Push-ups, laps, dribbles, throws, and a game of Skins and Shirts in which the players were constantly changing. Coach Davidson was never very happy with their efforts and never overlooked the opportunity to share that opinion with the boys.

Jonathan tried to ignore the coach's sarcastic comments. Even when he said, "Rossi, I've seen pigs fly better than you throw," Jonathan had only gritted his teeth and nodded, vowing to himself to do better.

When one of the fifth graders quit the team, Ham, who always looked like a bright red tomato at the end of each practice session, had some things to confide to Jonathan.

Mrs. Volini's class was in the library to research their social-studies topics. The papers weren't even due until after Christmas vacation, so the kids were milling around or sitting at tables with books in their hands. Mostly, they were just talking.

Ham and Jonathan were standing alone at the far end of the library, pretending they were looking at the big globe that stood waist-high in the corner instead of just spinning it around. "I swear, Jon," Ham said, "I don't know how long I can keep this up."

"Your passing is getting much better," Jonathan said encouragingly.

Ham drummed his fingers against Europe. "But all that running. And those push-ups." Ham shuddered.

"Maybe you'll lose some weight."

"I'm not fat," Ham said huffily. "I'm broad. My dad says all the men in our family are broad."

Jonathan thought of Ham's father, who was as wide as he was tall. He was broad all right.

"Besides"—Ham's voice was firm—"I don't like that Davidson guy."

"You don't have to like him. The way he talks to us, he's just trying to motivate us."

"Motivate us? What does that mean?"

"Get us going. A lot of coaches motivate their teams by yelling at them and saying they're worthless," Jonathan explained.

"Coach Davidson's got motivating down real good," said Ham dispiritedly.

Jonathan tried again. "Don't you see, Ham? The coach tells us how bad we are, and then we want to do better."

Ham looked at Jonathan with troubled eyes. "When the coach tells me I'm an out-of-shape mess, I just want to quit."

Jonathan thought about this. He read a lot

about sports, and he knew what Coach Davidson was doing wasn't unusual at all. It happened in college and professional sports all the time. But motivation was supposed to make you try harder. Never in all Jonathan's reading had it made someone give up.

"Look, the first game is coming up," Jonathan finally said. "We're going to be out on the court against the South Lake Indians in our new uniforms. You wouldn't want to miss that."

Ham sighed. "I guess not. I hope we win, though. Coach Davidson will kill us if we don't."

"Then your problem would be solved," Jonathan said philosophically.

Finally, Ham laughed. "Thanks, but I'd rather stay alive. At least until the dance."

Jonathan stood up a little straighter. "Have you asked anybody yet?"

Ham looked down at the globe as if finding India was the only thing on his mind. "Not yet."

"Well, you'd better hurry up. All the good girls are going to be gone. Who do you want to ask?"

Ham shrugged. "I don't know."

Then Jonathan had a brilliant idea. "Why don't you ask Sharon? She's Robin's best friend, and then we could go together."

When Ham didn't say anything, Jonathan looked at him, perplexed. "Is there someone else you wanted to go with?"

"I guess Veronica Volner wouldn't go with me," Ham said shyly.

Jonathan couldn't believe his ears. Veronica Volner was the most stuck-up girl in the sixth grade. Why would Ham want to go with her? "You don't like Veronica, do you?"

"She's neat," Ham said, staring off into space.

"But she can be so mean. Remember how she treated Robin?" At the beginning of the school year, Robin and Veronica had been best friends, until they had had a fight and Veronica had turned all the girls against her. Robin had turned the situation around, but Jonathan still got a tight, hard feeling in his throat when he thought of Veronica.

"Yeah, I know, but still, it would really be something to go to the dance with Veronica."

Despite his feelings about her, Jonathan knew what Ham meant. Veronica had a way about her that caused people to pay attention.

Well liked or not, she had status, and so would any boy that took her to the dance. Jonathan shrugged. "It's up to you, I guess."

Ham looked startled. "You mean I should ask her?"

"That's the only way you'll ever find out if she'll go with you. There she is." Jonathan pointed out Veronica sitting a few tables away, looking through a magazine, her finger idly playing with her long dark hair.

"Now?"

"She's alone. All she can say is no."

Ham started tearing up bits of notebook paper. "That's what I'm afraid of."

"Then forget it. I don't like her, anyway."

Ham looked longingly in Veronica's direction.

"Nah . . . I'll ask her."

Gathering his courage, he brushed a few tiny pieces of paper off his pants and walked over to Veronica.

Jonathan watched as Ham sat down beside Veronica. With a smile pasted on his face, Ham began to speak.

Veronica wrinkled her nose. Then she started talking and waving her arms about. Ham kept nodding, but his smile melted away. Finally, he got up and went back to Jonathan.

"So what did she say?" Jonathan demanded.

Ham looked as tired as if he had just finished a basketball practice. "It was a little complicated."

"What do you mean? She must have given you some kind of an answer."

"She said a bunch of stuff. Like that the dance was pretty important. And that she had to be careful before she accepted an invitation. She told me she couldn't go with just anyone."

Jonathan wasn't surprised. "Typical Veronica. So how did you leave it?"

Ham looked over in Veronica's direction. "She said she'd let me know, but for now she was going to wait."

"Wait? For what?"

"She was pretty clear about that. She's waiting for a better offer."

C H A P T E R
FIVE

Jonathan stood in the corner of the gym, peering at the crowded bleachers. He picked out his parents, which wasn't hard to do. His mother was wearing a bright blue sweater, and his father was gesturing animatedly as he talked. Even David had agreed to honor the Wildcats with his presence, though he had balked about going to a middle school game until he found out that Mike Stone's older sister would be there, too. David and Amanda Stone were deep in conversation in the first row.

Farther up, a little to the right, were Robin and Sharon. Robin was looking around the gym, and Jonathan knew she was looking for him. When she found him, she waved, and Jonathan, after checking to see that none of his teammates were watching, waved back.

"Hey, you'd better keep your mind on the game, not on your girlfriend," Mike hissed in his ear.

Jonathan gave him a disgusted look. "Worry about yourself. You haven't looked so hot in practice."

"I've been making baskets," Mike said indignantly.

"Yeah, but you weren't playing against anyone at the time. Now we have opponents." He pointed to the corner of the gym where the South Lake Indians were huddled together.

"Aw, they don't look so tough."

Jonathan had to agree. The Wildcats didn't look all that great in their new green uniforms, but the Indians looked worse. Colored an unfortunate shade of yellow, the Indians' uniforms hung on the boys, making them look even smaller than most of the fifth-grade Wildcats.

"We'll whip 'em," Jonathan said, nodding his head. "No problem."

But once the whistle blew and the teams were on the court, it was practically impossible to tell the Indians from the Wildcats—

from their skill levels, anyway. Jonathan figured the other players, including Mike at forward and Ham at guard, would feed him the ball for easy lay-ups, as he had seen happen so many times on television. As the game progressed, however, one thing was immediately clear: This didn't look like any basketball he had ever seen on TV.

Jonathan could see that he wasn't going to be on the receiving end of any nifty lob passes. No, if he was going to touch the ball at all, he'd have to go get it for himself. When Ham was caught in a corner surrounded by three Indians and looking frantically for something to do with the ball, Jonathan managed to run up beside him and yell, "Ham, over here!" Admittedly, the pass Ham threw looked more like a football handoff, but at least the result was right—Jonathan got the ball.

Now what? He was at least ten feet from the basket and his four teammates were all yelling, "Rossi, I'm open!" As near as Jonathan could tell, though, they were all stretching the truth. When he looked over the head of the gawky Indian attempting to guard him, all he could see was a mass of Indians and Wildcats, a nine-headed monster that craved basketballs. Passing was clearly out, and attempting to dribble seemed equally unwise. With no choices left, he attempted a shot, firing away with two hands over the Indians' waving arms. The shot banged wildly off the backboard and rebounded straight back into Jonathan's hands. More surprised than anything else, Jonathan shot again—and missed.

Jonathan thought that play might be the game's most embarrassing moment, but he was wrong. Much worse was when Ham got mixed up and started dribbling the ball in the wrong direction. The Indians were so startled, they didn't even attempt to guard him, so Ham moved leisurely down the court and, with a greater ease than he had ever shown in practice, tossed the ball into the hoop.

There was an elated look on Ham's face as he turned around, waiting for the cheers of the crowd. The utter silence confused him until Mike found his voice and yelled, "Wrong way, you hamburger."

Elation turned quickly to horror. Ham, not knowing what else to do, just stood under the basket. A whistle blew, and Jonathan ran over to him.

"I didn't do that," Ham moaned.

"Yeah, you did," Jonathan said, trying to hide his exasperation.

The referee walked to the middle of the court and blew his whistle again. "The shot was made in the wrong basket. Score two points for the Indians."

Jonathan glared at Ham, who wouldn't meet his eyes. Two points to the other team! It made Jonathan want to walk off the court right there, but he kept on playing, and finally it paid off when he made a basket. Before the half was over, Mike had made one, too. They were winning, but four to two wasn't a very impressive score.

Coach Davidson didn't think so, either. He had already pulled Ham off the court and had given him a talking to so fierce, Davidson's face was redder than Ham's had ever been after practice. During the half, it was everyone else's turn. He gathered the boys around him, his face stern. "I don't like what I'm seeing out there."

"We're winning, aren't we?" Mike muttered.

The coach whirled in Mike's direction. "Not by much. In fact, I don't know when I've ever seen a lower-scoring game. Michael Jordan can get four points with both hands tied behind his back," he added, his voice dripping with sarcasm.

Jonathan doubted that Michael Jordan, the Bulls' most valuable player, would be caught dead playing for the Forest Glen Wildcats.

"Now I want to see more out there in the third period."

Jonathan assumed he meant more scoring, as opposed to more guys running the wrong way down the court.

There was more scoring in the third period, but it was the Indians who were doing it. Jonathan didn't know what speech their coach had given them during the half, but something seemed to have set the Indians on fire. Suddenly, there were skinny little kids everywhere, passing, shooting, and making baskets. By the end of the third period, the Indians were winning, twelve to seven. Paul, Mike, and Jonathan each scored in the fourth period, but the Indians added one field goal and two free throws. The game ended with the Indians winning, sixteen to thirteen.

The locker room was quiet after the Wildcat loss. After the boys had finished showering and dressing, Coach Davidson called them together.

"Not another speech," Mike whispered as they walked to the spot where Coach Davidson stood, his arms folded, his face like granite.

"I just want to go home," Jonathan answered, although facing his father wasn't a very pleasing prospect, either. Jonathan looked around for Ham. He was lagging behind the rest of the team, his head down. As the boys gathered in a circle, Ham stood on the outside, his arms folded, just like Coach Davidson.

"I'm not going to say much," Coach Davidson said through clenched lips.

The word *good* was written on the face of every Wildcat.

"But if you think you're going to look this bad at your next game, you're sadly mistaken. You think we've been practicing hard up until now? You haven't seen anything yet. Now go home and get a good night's sleep. You're going to need it. Starting tomorrow."

The boys looked at one another. Tomorrow was Saturday.

"That's right, tomorrow. At ten o'clock sharp. I've arranged with Mr. Thomas for Saturday practices when needed. I think we can all agree one is needed. Now get out of here."

When they were out of Coach Davidson's earshot, Paul moaned loudly. "My mother rescheduled my piano lessons from Monday to

Saturday. She is going to have one major-league hissy fit."

"Would you rather explain the problem to her or to the coach?" Mike growled.

Paul pushed his glasses up on his nose. "I'll talk to her."

The team began leaving the locker room; nobody wanted to linger there. But Jonathan fell back to where Ham was shuffling along. Ham looked so pathetic, Jonathan couldn't stay angry. He flung one arm around his friend's shoulder. "Hey, cheer up. Things aren't so bad."

Ham shook off the arm and looked at him fiercely. "Right. I didn't score once, I tripped over my shoelace during the third period, and I shot a basket into the wrong hoop. And you tell me things aren't so bad."

There was no point in making Ham feel worse than he already did. "Everyone has probably forgotten that by now," Jonathan said soothingly.

"Hey, look, it's Backwards Berger." Two sixth-grade boys snickered as Jonathan and Ham entered the almost-empty gym.

Ham groaned. "Not another nickname."

Jonathan saw his parents waving frantically

from the near-empty stands. "I've got to go. Do you need a ride home?"

"No. My mom's waiting outside for me."

"Okay." Jonathan stood, wavering. "Don't let it get to you."

Ham just shrugged and turned toward the door.

All thoughts of Ham's problem flew from Jonathan's head like moths from a closet the moment he was close enough to the stands to hear his father's voice.

"Jonathan, what was going on with you guys?"

Mrs. Rossi put a restraining hand on her husband's shoulder. "Not here."

"I didn't like what I saw out there," he said, practically quoting Coach Davidson.

Now Jonathan could see that his father's eyebrows were knit tightly together.

"Me, either, Dad," he said with a sigh.

"Here's your jacket, dear," Mrs. Rossi said, trying to keep her tone light. "David took a ride with the Stones."

Jonathan raised his eyes to where Robin had been sitting, but she and Sharon were gone.

It was a long ride home. Jonathan would have sworn his house had moved several miles farther from the school. How else was there time for his father to go over every play, critique every player? Jonathan, too, came in for his fair share of pointed comments.

"You weren't paying attention, Jon. You have to be able to put some moves on the guys covering you. You were running right into them." He blasted the horn when the light turned green and the car in front of him didn't move quickly enough.

Jonathan stared out the window.

"And you had at least two other opportunities to score. You've got to learn how to use your hands."

His mother turned around and patted one of the offending appendages.

"Are you listening to me?" Mr. Rossi glared at Jonathan in the rearview mirror.

Did he have a choice? Jonathan knew better than to voice that thought, though. Instead, he said, "You know, Dad, I did score a lot of the points."

Mr. Rossi snorted. "There were only thirteen of them all told."

"Come on now, Mitch," Mrs. Rossi said to her husband. "This was Jonathan's first game."

"All right," Mr. Rossi muttered. "But next

time, he'll have to do better. Practice harder."

"We have another practice tomorrow morning."

"On Saturday?" Mrs. Rossi asked with raised eyebrows.

At least his mother felt sorry for him. "Yeah, first thing."

"It seems this Coach Davidson is working you boys awfully hard."

"He has to," Mr. Rossi responded, "if he doesn't want another debacle on his hands."

Jonathan wasn't sure what a debacle was, but if it was anything like a humiliating loss, his father was probably right.

Although Jonathan arrived at the gym promptly at ten o'clock the next morning, Mike and some of the other boys were already tossing the ball around, under Coach Davidson's watchful eye. The coach wasn't saying much, merely barking out orders, and occasional short, sharp criticisms. Soon, most of the boys, even Paul, were on the court, but Ham was nowhere to be seen.

After practice started, Jonathan didn't have time to worry about Ham. Push-ups were kids' stuff compared to the drills Coach Davidson had come up with for this morning. Losing seemed to inspire him. After a full round of calisthenics, the coach gathered the team together at half court.

"I want you to think about one thing today," he declared. "Defense."

That seemed odd to Jonathan. The Wildcats had proved yesterday that they couldn't shoot, pass, or dribble. So why weren't they working on offense? After all, the Indians had scored only sixteen points.

Coach Davidson explained. "Shooting drills are too much fun for a team that played as badly as you guys. What you need is discipline, and you get discipline from defense. Besides, anyone can play defense . . . anyone who is willing to work."

Jonathan wasn't so sure about that. Wanting to do something didn't seem to be enough, at least on the basketball court. His doubts were even stronger after ten minutes of the "shuffle" drill.

"When you play defense," the coach instructed as he explained the drill, "you need to have a low center of gravity. That means keeping your butt down."

For a moment, Jonathan thought the coach had actually meant to say something funny, but the glare he gave to a fifth grader who tittered at the word *butt* convinced him otherwise.

"As the man you're guarding moves to his right or left, shuffle your legs to keep up with him. Don't let your legs cross. Keep your eyes on your man at all times. Okay, let's try it."

As the coach dribbled a ball first to the right and then to the left, the players grouped into lines, shuffled after him, changing direction when he did.

"Hey, Rossi," Mike whispered from behind him, "is this stupid or what? It's almost like one of those dumb folk dances we do in gym."

Jonathan quickly nodded, not wanting to let the coach see him, but, like Mike, he was puzzled as to why they were wasting their time on such a sissy drill.

Four minutes later, Jon had changed his mind about the sissy part. Eight minutes later, he knew he was going to die at any second. Ten minutes later, collapsed in a heap on the gym floor along with his teammates, he wasn't dead, but he wished he were.

"Shuffle drill was a little harder than you thought, eh?" Coach Davidson asked with satisfaction in his voice. "Now we're going to run laps." He started pointing at boys and calling out names and numbers. "Wolfe, twenty laps; Marks, eighteen; Rossi, thirty."

As the boys ran, the coach yelled in a strong loud voice, "I may not be able to keep you from losing, but you're going to be in shape and you're going to know how to play defense. Got that?"

Jonathan got it. He kept running, counted his laps, and then wondered whether anybody was actually running as many as they were supposed to. At twenty-three, he trudged off the court along with Mike, who was pretending to be finishing his nineteenth trip around the gym.

As they neared the locker-room door, Coach Davidson called Jonathan back. How could he know how many laps I ran? Jonathan thought anxiously. That wasn't what was on the coach's mind, however.

"Berger had better have a good reason for not being here. I suggest you tell him that."

Jonathan looked up at the coach. His face seemed miles away. "I will," he said softly, but inside he was mad. Why did he have to be the one to give Ham the bad news?

*   *   *

He worried about it as he hurried home. His parents were gone, but David was sitting at the kitchen table eating a bologna sandwich. They had missed each other last night and Jonathan eyed him warily. "Okay, go ahead, say it."

David shook his head. "Not me," he said, though his words were a little hard to make out because his mouth was full.

Jonathan sat down across from him and helped himself to a piece of bread from the loaf. He also took several pieces of bologna from the package, put the meat in the bread, and folded the whole thing in half and took a bite. It wasn't pretty, but it tasted good. "So how come you're not going to rag me?"

"First of all, I figure you heard all you needed to from Dad."

"True."

"Second, I know how it is to have a lousy first game."

Jonathan looked at his brother suspiciously. He was being awfully nice.

"Third, I need you to lend me two dollars."

The light dawned. "Uh-uh," Jonathan said, shaking his head. "I shouldn't have to pay you just for staying off my back."

"That's right," David admitted. "But will you loan it to me anyway?"

Jonathan considered. "What will you do for me? Besides pay it back, I mean?"

"I'll change the subject every time Dad brings up the game."

"Deal," Jonathan said.

After lunch, Jonathan went over to Robin's. He would have liked to have stayed home and taken a long nap, but Bobby was going to be there, too, to discuss the Battle of the Books. The three of them had decided to form a team.

"Hi," Robin said as she flung open the door. Jonathan hoped that Robin wasn't going to say anything about last night's loss, but the first words out of her mouth were "Sorry about the game."

Jonathan didn't know where to look. In his fantasies, Robin had always been looking at him adoringly, admiring his skill with a basketball. He had never visualized her with this look of pity on her face.

"Oh, we'll get better," he said, trying to sound confident.

"Sure you will," she replied as she led Jonathan into her cozy book-filled sun room.

Bobby was already seated on the couch, pouring over the list of books the librarian had handed out yesterday. Jonathan hoped he wouldn't have to listen to any condolences from Bobby, but apparently he hadn't heard about the game or didn't care. All he said to Jonathan was "Hi."

"So are we ready to get started?" Jonathan asked, settling himself on a worn leather recliner.

"We will be when we read these books. It's a lot of work," Bobby said bluntly, handing the list of books over to Jonathan.

Jonathan had gotten the list yesterday at school. His mind had been on the game, so he had just stuffed it into his notebook. Now, he took the time to look it over. There were two pages of titles.

"Miss Morris won't start the battles until the first of the year," Robin said, "but if we're a team, we've got to start reading now."

Suddenly, Jonathan felt his stomach knot nervously. How was he going to have time to do all this extra reading and practice, too? When Bobby suggested they all form a team, it seemed like a great way to do two things he liked—hanging around with Robin and reading some decent books. Now, however, confronted with a list of thirty titles, Jonathan felt overwhelmed.

"Jonathan?"

Jonathan focused on Robin, who looked as if she was waiting for an answer. "What?"

"I asked which of these books you want to start with."

Before Jonathan could answer, Bobby said, "I think we should each take ten and then trade off."

"Is that okay, Jon?" Robin asked.

"Oh sure," Jonathan said, trying to look confident. "I can handle it. No problem." Mentally, though, he was shaking his head. Ten books. It might as well be ten thousand.

CHAPTER
SIX

Mrs. Volini was late. Mr. Thomas came in to tell the class that she was having car trouble and that they should just sit quietly until she arrived. Impressed that they were being left to look after themselves, the class made an unspoken decision to be on their best behavior. That didn't mean sitting with their hands folded. Knots of kids were standing or sitting around all over the room talking, but they were doing it quietly. The sixth grade was smart enough to know just how loud they could get without Mr. Thomas making another appearance.

Jonathan had been calling Ham all weekend with no success. That morning, he had waited in the school yard until the last possible moment, but Ham never showed. Finally, Ham slid into his seat as the sound of the last bell was fading away.

Now that everyone was getting up and walking around, Jonathan went over to where Ham was sitting with his nose buried in his history book.

"What are you doing, Ham?" Jonathan asked. "Our history test isn't until Wednesday."

"So?" Ham replied defensively. "Can't I get a head start?"

"Sure." Ham never studied until the last minute, though. "I've been trying to get hold of you. You missed practice." Jonathan didn't mention that Coach Davidson was also interested in Ham's reasons for missing practice.

Ham reluctantly closed his book. "I didn't feel like going. Then my gram called and said she was lonely, so we went up to Wisconsin to see her." He sighed. "I wish we could have stayed all week."

"I told you to forget about the game."

"That's easy," Ham said sarcastically. "Especially since I'm the laughingstock of Kennedy Middle School."

"Come on, it's not that bad. You've been in school only five minutes."

Ham gave him a piercing look.

"Okay, so it will be bad for a while. Then everyone will forget about it. You'll make up for it at the next game."

"There's not going to be a next game." Ham slammed his book down on the desk. "I'm quitting."

Jonathan shook his head. "No way, Ham."

"I've decided," Ham said vehemently.

"I'm not going to let you be a quitter!"

"Why not?"

"Because," Jonathan sputtered, "because it's not right."

Robin joined Jonathan at Ham's desk. "What's not right?" she asked.

"Ham says he's quitting the team."

Robin looked embarrassed. "Oh."

"So tell him he can't do it."

"Who says I can't?" Ham demanded.

"My dad says. Everybody says." Jonathan turned to Robin. "You just don't drop something in the middle. Isn't that true?"

Robin examined the sleeve of her sweater. "Well . . ."

Jonathan racked his brain to think of a saying of his father's. Finally, it came to him. "Ham, when the going gets tough, the tough get going."

Ham's round features wrinkled into a disgusting face, and then he stuck his finger down his throat and pretended to gag. Jonathan could feel himself getting angry.

"Oh sure, just be a jerk about it," he retorted.

Ham's shoulders sagged, and he said sadly, "Look, I don't like basketball as much as I thought I would. I've had a stomachache since that stupid game. I don't want to walk around with a stomachache until the basketball season is over."

Before Jonathan could respond, Robin said, "I don't blame you. If you want to quit, Ham, then you should."

Jonathan's expression was murderous. "Robin . . ."

"You can't make him stay on the team."

Ham brightened a bit. "That's right. You can't make me."

"Robin, why are you taking his side?" Jonathan demanded.

She didn't answer right away. Then she said, "I guess because what Ham wants to do is all that matters."

Before Jonathan could say anything else, Robin went back to her seat.

"Listen, Jon," Ham said, trying to get

Jonathan's attention away from Robin, "there is one thing about quitting the team."

"Yeah?"

"I don't want to be the one to tell Coach Davidson."

"I don't blame you," Jonathan said meanly.

"He's going to call me a quitter like you did," Ham said. "And maybe some other stuff, too."

"Probably." Jonathan knew he wasn't being very nice, but he really did want Ham to stay on the team. Even if Ham never got any better, just having him around was fun.

Ham looked at Jonathan earnestly. "That's why I thought you might tell him for me."

"Me?" Jonathan looked at him in disbelief. "No way." He turned away and started walking down the aisle, "Uh-uh."

Ham scrambled after him. "Just tell him I twisted my ankle and can't play."

Jonathan didn't even glance back. "No." Then he stopped suddenly and faced Ham, who almost ran into him. "If you're going to do it, then do it yourself."

Ham stared at Jonathan for a moment and then defiantly said, "All right, I will."

Jonathan and Ham barely spoke during lunch. Apparently having made up his mind to talk to the coach, Ham was able to ignore the gibes from the other guys about his basketball playing. He didn't tell them he was quitting, though.

Jonathan wondered all afternoon whether he had done the right thing by denying Ham's request. When Mrs. Volini started talking about moral dilemmas after lunch, he wondered even more. Ham was his friend. He could have passed his message along to the coach. Did he say no because he thought Ham should take responsibility for his own actions? Or was he as afraid of Coach Davidson as Ham was?

Mrs. Volini pushed a strand of hair back into her bun. "Have any of you come up against any situations lately where you've had to make uncomfortable choices?"

Jonathan lowered his eyes. Sometimes it worked: If you pretended to be invisible, Mrs. Volini didn't call on you. A sigh of relief slipped from Jonathan's lips as he heard Mrs. Volini call on Candy Dahl, who prattled on about her decision to borrow her sister's sweater without telling her. Mrs. Volini informed Candy that that didn't qualify as a moral dilemma.

He wasn't safe for long, though. "Jonathan?"

With a snap of his head, Jonathan stared up at Mrs. Volini.

"Yes?"

"Do you have anything you'd like to share with us?"

Squirming a little, Jonathan replied, "Uh, not me."

"You know, you're supposed to be thinking about these issues for your composition."

"I know." Jonathan racked his brain for something, anything, that would prove he'd been thinking about moral issues—other than the one that had been occupying him today. "My cousin's coming to visit," Jonathan began. "I don't have much in common with him."

"That sounds more like a social problem," Mrs. Volini said.

Jonathan warmed to his subject. "Yeah, but should I be nice to him even though he's a drag? Or should I let him ruin my Thanksgiving vacation?"

"I see what you mean," Mrs. Volini said thoughtfully. "Well, class, what is our obligation to other people? How do we decide whether it's more important to extend ourselves to others or to do what we like?"

The class was off and running, but Jonathan didn't pay much attention. He already knew he was going to have to be nice to Mark. His mother would kill him if he wasn't.

When it was time for practice, Jonathan walked into the gym with trepidation. The first thing he saw was Ham deep in conversation with Coach Davidson at the sidelines. Jonathan lingered near the door to the locker room, trying to overhear, but with no success. Ham had seen him, though, and the moment he was finished, he bounded over to Jonathan.

"He canned me," Ham said happily.

"What!"

"Before I could say anything, he went into this long speech about not having what it takes, and how some people aren't suited for certain activities."

"And he told you you had to quit the team?"

"Not exactly. He said I could ride the bench if I wanted to, or be a backup player, but I just said I didn't want to." Ham's smile was generous. "We both pretended to be down about it, but Davidson was just as happy as I was. Maybe happier."

Despite his wanting Ham to stay on the team, Jonathan felt relief wash over him. Ham got his way and neither one of them had to give the news to Davidson. Ham, always so quick to forget any squabble, didn't even seem to care that Jonathan had refused to get him off the hook. "I guess Davidson will have to find someone else to play guard," Jonathan said.

Ham wrinkled his forehead. "Guard?"

It was clear to Jonathan that Ham's mind was officially no longer on basketball.

"Yeah, you know, the position you played until two minutes ago."

Ham giggled. "I know. I was just trying to remember what Davidson said about the new player."

Jonathan leaned forward. "What new player?"

"I don't know his name. Davidson just said something about a new kid coming after Thanksgiving and that he had been a hotshot at his old school."

"Well, that should be good for the team," Jonathan said uncertainly. He wondered just how talented this kid was.

"Yep," Ham said cheerfully. "You guys stink."

Jonathan punched him in the shoulder. "Oh, so now it's 'you guys'? We're still your school's team, don't forget. Besides, we're going to get better. Coach Davidson will see to that," Jonathan added grimly.

*   *   *

To Jonathan's amazement, during the next couple of practice sessions, the Wildcats didn't improve. They got even worse.

This went contrary to everything Jonathan thought he knew about sports. You practice, and you get better. He had certainly never heard of anyone trying really hard and getting worse. Jonathan would have liked to ask his father about this phenomenon, but Jonathan didn't want him to know how badly he was playing. He decided to ask David, and caught him before breakfast when he was brushing his teeth. It was the day before Thanksgiving, and the Wildcats would be playing their second game that night.

"Say, Dave," Jonathan began casually. "When's your last game?"

David answered through a mouthful of toothpaste. "Two weeks from Saturday."

"How do you think your team is going to wind up?"

"Our last two games are pretty easy. We should win them, so we'll be six and four."

"So your team got better as the season went on," Jonathan said, slamming down the lid of the toilet and taking a seat.

David looked at Jonathan curiously. "Yeah. Why?"

Jonathan shrugged. "I dunno. I think our team is getting worse. Is that possible?"

David rinsed. Then he said, "Sure, if your players don't have any talent."

"We have talent," Jonathan bristled.

"How are you doing?" David asked pointedly.

Jonathan hesitated. Should he tell his brother the truth? "I'm having some trouble," he finally admitted.

David eyed him critically. "Well, you're tall enough. How's your ball-handling?"

"A little rough. I just can't seem to put everything together."

"You're only playing your second game. Give it time."

"But we're always practicing, and Davidson just never lets up on us. That wouldn't be so bad, if I was seeing some results . . ." His voice trailed off.

"Maybe basketball's not your game. When you get to high school, you can try football."

"But it's the basketball team I'm on now," Jonathan said in a defeated tone.

He felt even more down after the game that evening. This time, the Wildcats lost big, and Jonathan had a hard time remembering whether he had done anything right. Coach Davidson certainly hadn't come up with any compliments in his little talk after the game. The only bright spot was that his dad, working late at the office so he'd have the whole holiday weekend off, wasn't around to critique his performance.

The smell of roasting turkey woke Jonathan up the next morning. For a few moments, he lay curled up in his warm bed, thinking of his mother's biscuits and pumpkin pie. Then other thoughts began to intrude: the fouls he had made, Coach Davidson's frown whenever his eyes lit on Jonathan.

Jonathan rolled over and bunched his blanket around him. He shut his eyes tight, but he couldn't wish himself back to sleep. Finally, Jonathan threw off his covers and sat up. What the heck, he thought. Next time I wake up, I'll just have to remember all over again that we lost.

The floor was cold when Jonathan got out of bed, and as usual, he couldn't find his slippers. Yesterday's smelly socks lay curled in a ball at the foot of his bed. He put them on and went downstairs.

"Jonathan, you're not dressed!" his mother exclaimed when he appeared in the kitchen a few minutes later.

He looked down at his pajamas. "I know."

Mrs. Rossi looked harried. She stacked a few more bowls in the sink, on what was already a virtual leaning tower. "Don't you want to go to the airport with your father to pick up Mark and Aunt Janice?"

Jonathan was startled. He was sure his father had already left by now, and on the way downstairs, he had been congratulating himself on missing him. "No, I don't want to go."

"That isn't very friendly." Mrs. Rossi paused. "Or isn't it Mark you don't want to see?"

"I . . . I thought I could get started on my reading for Battle of the Books."

"That's fine, Jon." His mother looked at him intently. "I just hope you're not avoiding your father."

"Where is Dad?"

"Picking up a few things I forgot at the store."

"I'll catch him later." Then he went upstairs and attempted to take the world's longest shower. When he emerged, knowing how a fish must feel, he felt sure that he had successfully evaded his dad—for a while, anyway.

Jonathan was carefully setting the table with his mother's best china when his Aunt Janice and Cousin Mark arrived. During the flurry of hellos, Jonathan eyed Mark. He didn't seem much older than he had when Jonathan had seen him at their grandmother's funeral two years ago. Skinny, sporting a bad haircut, and with a mouthful of braces, Mark could only be described in one word—*wimpy*. Jonathan sighed. Suddenly, the holiday weekend stretched endlessly ahead.

Before they sat down to eat, the moment Jonathan had been dreading arrived. His father pulled him aside and said, "Your mother told me you lost last night."

"Yeah, we did," Jonathan admitted.

"What happened?" Mr. Rossi asked with a sigh.

Jonathan didn't know what he was supposed to say—that everybody played badly, and that he played worst of all? "I guess it just wasn't our night," he finally responded.

His father ran his fingers through his thick hair. "I don't get it. You're practicing all the time. I know you're trying, Jon."

"I don't get it, either," Jonathan muttered.

"Well, you're just going to have to keep at it." Mr. Rossi patted his son's shoulder. "Practice makes perfect."

Jonathan knew he would be happy if practice just made average. Mr. Rossi launched into a series of moves he wanted Jonathan to work on, but he was interrupted by Aunt Janice, who came up to them and said, "Sorry to interrupt, Mitch, but dinner is served."

Jonathan was ready to take his usual place at the table when Mrs. Rossi said brightly, "Jon, why don't you sit next to Mark. I'm sure you two boys have a lot to talk about."

Mark and Jonathan looked at each other warily, but they took their assigned seats. Despite Mrs. Rossi's hopes, however, the only words they spoke during dinner were phrases that began with the words, *Please pass the* . . .

Finally, Mr. Rossi pushed himself away from the table with a groan. "I couldn't eat another bite."

"Me, either," Aunt Janice agreed. "It was a wonderful dinner, Anne."

"Thank you," Mrs. Rossi said. She got up and began clearing.

Mr. Rossi got up, too. "Well, I guess that's our cue to watch some football, hey guys?"

Aunt Janice looked shocked. "But Anne cooked the dinner, Mitch."

"I know." He turned to his wife. "It was great, honey."

"That's not what I meant—"

"It's all right, Janice," Mrs. Rossi interrupted.

"No it isn't. You spent all day cooking, and we should help you clean up."

"Fine." Mr. Rossi scooped up a few plates and carried them awkwardly into the kitchen.

"You know," Aunt Janice continued, as she scraped plates at the dining room table, "in my house, one person cooks, and the other person cleans up. We trade off."

Jonathan threw an astonished look in Mark's direction. Mark actually cooked? The only thing Jonathan could do was use the microwave.

Mr. Rossi returned from the kitchen just in time to hear Aunt Janice's comment. He rolled his eyes upward, as if he was asking heaven for patience. Grabbing a few glasses, he carried them out to the sink. Then he drifted back through the dining room toward the den. David followed him.

Aunt Janice looked over at Mrs. Rossi, who shrugged.

Jonathan knew he could leave, too, but Mark was still helping to clear the table. Besides, his mother had gotten up awfully early to start fixing the dinner. It seemed only fair to help out a little, so he took the empty sweet-potato casserole into the kitchen.

"You shouldn't let him get away with it," Aunt Janice said loudly.

"Oh, Janice, I'm trying to raise the boys differently, but let's face it, Mitch is set in his ways."

Jonathan didn't want to hear this conversation. He ran the water loudly over the dishes as he scraped the uneaten bits of food into the garbage disposal. Mark came up behind him and set a few more plates down on the counter with a clatter.

"You scared me," Jonathan said accusingly.

"Sorry."

He didn't look very sorry, Jonathan thought. "Is your mom always like that?"

Mark leaned against the dishwasher. "Like what?"

"Well . . ." Jonathan didn't want to be rude. "Does she always just speak her mind like that?"

"Always."

Mrs. Rossi came in carrying what was left of

the turkey. "I'm glad to see you boys getting along so well."

Jonathan cringed. He and Mark had said barely ten words to each other, and his mother already assumed they were buddies. Mark probably thought they were buddies, too, but when Jonathan glanced over at him, Mark was simply looking embarrassed.

Aunt Janice joined them, her hands full of silverware and dirty napkins. "I swear, a Thanksgiving dinner is unbelievable. It takes a day to shop for, a day to cook, and a half hour to eat."

"At least we didn't have to kill the turkey like we used to." Mrs. Rossi laughed.

"When did you ever kill a turkey?" Jonathan asked.

Mrs. Rossi began wrapping up the leftovers. "You know we lived on a farm until I was twelve. We used to raise all our own poultry."

"And you really killed them?"

"Well, mostly your grandmother did," Mrs. Rossi said, "but every once in a while Janice and I had to do it."

"How? How did you kill them?" Mark demanded.

Mrs. Rossi didn't say anything. Finally, Aunt Janice replied, "Actually, we had to wring their necks."

Jonathan and Mark stared at each other in horror. "Oh, gross," Jonathan said.

"You're kidding, right, Mom?" Mark asked.

Aunt Janice laughed. "I can see we haven't told you boys enough about our days growing up on the farm."

So while they all loaded the dishwasher and stored the food, the women regaled the boys with stories of their childhood. Pretty soon, they were laughing about the first time Aunt Janice was allowed to collect eggs. Instead of taking them in the house, she had decided to see whether she could really fry an egg on the hot cement driveway.

"Well, I was just six at the time," Aunt Janice said, wiping the tears from her eyes.

"Was Grandma mad?" Mark asked.

"I'll say. Especially since I tried to fry every one of them."

Mrs. Rossi looked around the clean kitchen. "I guess many hands do make light work," she said. "This is certainly the fastest I've ever gotten things back together after a big holiday dinner. I thank all of you. Boys, do you want to go watch the game now?"

Jonathan wiped his finger around the edge of the counter. "I don't know." His dad was probably wondering why he hadn't made it into the den earlier, but he didn't feel like watching television for the rest of the afternoon. The best games weren't even on until the evening. "What do you want to do?" he asked Mark.

"I should practice my violin."

"You brought your violin?"

"Mark really has to practice every day. He has a recital coming up at Christmas," Aunt Janice answered for him.

"Oh, Jon, why don't you take Mark upstairs and listen to him practice," his mother said.

Jonathan felt stuck. He didn't want to watch football, but that had to be better than listening to Mark play the violin. Jonathan was all ready to say maybe he would join his dad and David when he caught his mother's eye.

Boy, Jonathan thought, averting his head, no one would ever have a moral dilemma if his mother was around. She always seemed to know the right thing to do. And she always wanted him to do it.

The silence was getting sweaty. Finally, Jonathan said, "Sure, you can play your fiddle up there if you want to."

"Violin," Mark corrected, but he followed Jonathan out of the kitchen.

As soon as they were alone in Jonathan's

room, the silence started up again. Jonathan didn't want to ask Mark to break it with a fiddle recital quite yet, so he was relieved when Mark started asking questions about the posters on the wall.

"Who's that?" Mark asked, pointing to the basketball player dribbling a ball on the back of Jonathan's closet door.

"Don't you ever look at your Wheaties box?"

"I don't eat Wheaties," Mark replied stiffly.

Jonathan rolled his eyes. "It's Michael Jordan. We'll be seeing him play tomorrow night when we go to the Bulls game."

"Oh." Mark sat down on the bottom bunk, where he would be sleeping.

"My dad went to a lot of trouble to get those tickets," Jonathan informed him.

Mark's smile was small. "I'll go. I just don't think your father likes me very much."

Jonathan didn't know what to say to that.

"Maybe it's because he knows I'm not interested in sports," Mark continued. "Or maybe it's because I don't really know how to talk to fathers."

"Hey, let me show you my basketball scrapbook . . ."

"You don't have to be embarrassed," Mark

110

said, staring at the Jordan poster. "It doesn't bother me that my dad left us."

"Do you ever see him?" Jonathan asked curiously.

"I've seen him a couple of times. He and Mom don't get along very well. I get postcards from him, though. Traveling around with the rodeo, he gets to see a lot of interesting places."

"Does he rope cows and stuff?"

Mark nodded. "He's won a couple of trophies for his riding."

"I can't imagine what it must be like having a father in the rodeo."

Mark's laugh was short and sharp. "I can't really imagine it, either."

"It's got to bother you a little bit, not having your dad around, I mean."

"Sometimes it does," Mark replied with a faraway look in his eyes. "In some ways, it's all right. Dads make me uncomfortable."

"Oh, that's just because you don't have one," Jonathan said, but he remembered there had been times when his own father had made him feel uncomfortable. "Do you miss him?" Jonathan asked.

Instead of answering, Mark leaned under

the lower bunk, where he had stashed his stuff, and pulled out his violin case. "Mind if I practice now?"

"Go ahead. I think I'll go downstairs and watch the game."

Before Jonathan could leave, Mark put his violin under his chin and started playing. Jonathan wasn't sure what he had expected, but it wasn't the heartbreaking music coming out of that violin. There was no way he could just walk away from it. It pulled him back.

The movement of Mark's arm as he pushed his bow back and forth over his instrument had its effect on Jonathan, too. For some reason, Jonathan thought of the graceful motions the best pitchers made as they threw the ball.

The music rolled on, finally reached a crescendo, and then ended. Mark put his bow and violin back in the case while Jonathan just stood there. Before he could decide how to voice his praise, Mark looked up at him.

"Yes, I guess sometimes I do miss my father," Mark said.

C H A P T E R

SEVEN

The visit was going better than Jonathan had expected. That night, full of turkey, tossing and turning in their bunks, Jonathan and Mark had some time to talk.

"So what's it like back there in San Francisco?" Jonathan asked.

"It's nice. Real pretty. It's too bad your family had to cancel your trip last summer."

"David got the chicken pox," Jonathan said with disgust.

"Maybe next summer. I'll show you Fisherman's Wharf, and there's a great zoo."

"We could even go to a Giants game." Then Jonathan wondered whether Mark had any interest in baseball, but Mark answered mildly,

"The A's are in Oakland. That's not very far at all. My girlfriend is a big A's fan."

"You have a girlfriend?" Jonathan tried to keep the surprise out of his voice.

"Sure, her name is Cindy."

"What's she like?"

That was all the invitation Mark needed. He launched into a description of Cindy, what she was like, how she looked, all of her hobbies. Cindy played the piano and she sometimes accompanied Mark at his recitals. Finally, Mark ran out of steam. "Do you have a girlfriend?" he asked.

Jonathan stared up at the ceiling. He hadn't felt comfortable with Robin after she had encouraged Ham to quit the team. Ham had been so happy about his decision, however, it didn't seem right for Jonathan to stay mad at Robin. By unspoken agreement, they had let the matter drop.

"So do you?" Mark asked again.

It was hard for him to talk about Robin, but he told Mark a little about her. "And she has a lot of common sense. I guess that sounds kind of stupid. I mean as a reason for liking a girl."

"I don't think it is. Cindy gives me a lot of good advice. My mom's great, but sometimes I don't want to talk to her. Or to any of the guys."

Jonathan knew just what Mark meant. Ham and Mike were a lot of fun, but their advice could be really lousy. A surprising thought crossed Jonathan's mind. Mark probably gave pretty good advice.

On Friday morning, the whole family went downtown. The day after Thanksgiving was the busiest shopping day of the year, and good-natured crowds filled the sidewalks. Finding a parking place wasn't easy, but once the group was out and walking around, everyone was glad that they had come.

It was warm for November, but fat Santas rang bells and called "Ho, Ho, Ho" as they stood in front of their kettles. Little children pressed their noses against department-store windows that were magic in miniature.

"Oh look," Aunt Janice said, pointing to one window. "It's a scene from *The Night Before Christmas.*"

" 'And Mamma in her kerchief, and I in my cap, Had just settled our brains for a long winter's nap,' " Mrs. Rossi quoted.

Jonathan elbowed his way closer to the scene, a gaily decorated living room, where the man and his wife stood nodding and smiling while huge snowflakes fell outside their window. Jonathan had loved these windows since he was a little boy, and he loved them now. He glanced up to see whether David thought he was being a baby, but David was smiling and looking at the windows, too.

It was too crowded to shop, but it was fun to be part of the bustle. They walked and walked until finally the adults pleaded that they were getting tired. "I wish we didn't have to go yet," Jonathan said, trying to catch a look at one festive window he had missed.

"Maybe we can stop for a few minutes on our way to the stadium tomorrow night," Mr. Rossi said.

The next morning, though, as everyone was sitting around the kitchen table having a leisurely breakfast, Aunt Janice noticed something in the newspaper.

"Mark! Simon Wilkerson is playing in Chicago tonight."

"Who's Simon Wilkerson?" Mr. Rossi asked, barely lifting his eyes from the financial section.

"He's a violinist," Mark answered. "One of the best."

"Do you think we could still get tickets for tonight?" Aunt Janice asked excitedly.

"Well, maybe you and I could go," Mrs.

Rossi said, "but Mitch did get the boys tickets for the basketball game."

Now Mr. Rossi looked up. "I'm sure if Mark prefers going to the concert, we could sell the ticket at the stadium. Or we could get one of the boys' friends to go along."

Everyone looked at Mark, who clearly felt he was on the spot. "I don't want to mess up anyone's plans," he said finally, "but I guess I'd like to go to the concert."

"Well, if he plays better than you, he must really be good," Jonathan said sincerely. He didn't expect Mark to turn to him and ask, "Would you like to go to the concert, too?"

Would he? Jonathan thought about it. After listening to Mark practice again last night, Jonathan knew he might like to attend a concert. Then he looked across the table at his dad's surprised expression. "Gee, I don't think so," he said.

David was already out of his seat. "I'm going to call Sam about Mark's ticket. Brian would take yours in a minute, Jon," he added.

"If you want to go to the concert, you should," Mrs. Rossi said quietly to Jonathan.

Mr. Rossi tried to keep his tone light. "It'll be a great game, Jon. But do whatever you want."

"No, Dad, I want to go with you," Jonathan said, panicking a little as he had when he was small and thought he was lost in a store. "Really."

Mr. Rossi picked up his newspaper. "Fine. Whatever you want."

Jonathan had been looking forward to the game, but now he felt mixed-up about going. He second-guessed his decision all through an outing to the Museum of Science and Industry. When he got to the game, however, he settled into his seat and tried to enjoy it.

It was disappointing, though. Two of the Bulls' best players were out, one with a pulled groin muscle, the other with the flu. And David's friend Sam was a major pain. He kept punching Jonathan in the side and saying stupid things like "Hey, Jonny, I bet you wish you could shoot like that."

Well, Jonathan thought, of course he did. But the Bulls' center wasn't five feet six and eleven years old. By the time he went home, Jonathan had a headache.

"How was the concert?" he asked Mark when they were alone upstairs in his room.

"Excellent," Mark said.

"What was it like?"

"It's a little hard to explain."

At first, Jonathan was hurt that Mark seemed so reluctant to share his evening. Then he realized that Simon Wilkerson's music was not the kind of thing you could simply describe. It would be like trying to explain clouds to someone who couldn't see.

Sunday afternoon, his mother took Aunt Janice and Mark to the airport. Once they had left, amid a flurry of thanks, Mr. Rossi peered out the window and said, "There's an hour of daylight, Jon. Why don't we go out and shoot some baskets?"

It would have been a perfect time to do some reading for the Battle of the Books, but Jonathan didn't want to disappoint his father. Dutifully, he got his basketball out of the garage and he and his dad went outside to shoot a few.

"I can't believe how warm it still is," Mr. Rossi said as he dribbled around the driveway.

Jonathan tried to steal the ball away from him. "I know. It hasn't gotten below forty yet."

While he was thinking about the weather, Mr. Rossi came off his dribble and faked a jump shot. Jonathan lurched into the air, trying to block the nonexistent shot, but Mr. Rossi effortlessly pivoted around him and Jonathan, off balance, was powerless to stop him. As he tried to regain his balance, Mr. Rossi's soft hook shot nestled quietly into the net.

"That's exactly what you've been doing wrong, Jon. You can't let the offensive player get you off your feet with a fake. Let's try it again."

This time, Mr. Rossi dribbled toward the hoop, with Jonathan guarding him. When his dad stopped his dribble and seemed ready to jump, Jonathan kept his feet firmly planted on the ground. His dad might think he was a lousy player, but he wasn't going to be fooled by the same move twice in a row. Except it didn't turn out to be the same move. This time, Jonathan's dad did jump, and with Jonathan steadfastly refusing to leave the ground, Mr. Rossi had no trouble sending a fifteen-foot shot through the net.

Jonathan could see that his father was forcing himself not to smile. But Mr. Rossi adopted a fatherly tone and said, "All right, let's try some jump shots now."

Oh sure, Jonathan thought. Jump shots. He might as well ask for a slam dunk.

Jump shot after jump shot produced nothing but disaster. Mr. Rossi became more frustrated with every futile attempt, and Jonathan more discouraged.

"No, Jon, no," Mr. Rossi called. "You've got to wait until you're at the top of your jump to shoot. Shooting on the way up is the baby way to do it. Do it again."

For some reason, Mr. Rossi still seemed convinced that Jonathan could be a good player. Jonathan seriously doubted this. He knew one thing for sure, though: Releasing his shot at the top of his jump was more important to his father than it was to him.

Finally, darkness came to Jonathan's rescue. "Isn't it getting kind of dark, Dad?" he asked tentatively.

"Oh, I guess you're right. Try one last jumper. This could be the one."

Trying to hide his lack of enthusiasm, Jonathan grabbed the ball, took a dribble, and attempted to launch yet another jump shot. This time, he actually did shoot at the top of his jump, but the ball thudded to the driveway, five feet short of the basket. Well, at least it wasn't the baby way, Jonathan thought bitterly.

Mr. Rossi grabbed the ball and fired a twenty-footer. Rubbing salt into Jonathan's wounds, the ball buried itself in the net.

"Nice shot, Dad," he forced himself to mutter.

Usually, after a practice session, Mr. Rossi gave Jonathan a full assessment of his performance. Today, however, he was quiet. Jonathan knew he should leave it alone but found himself asking out of habit, "How did I do?"

"Do you want the truth?" Mr. Rossi said as Jonathan followed him into the garage, where all their sports equipment was stored.

He didn't, but he answered, "Sure."

"You're not using your natural talent, Jon."

Stung, Jonathan headed for the house. "Maybe I just don't have any." Mr. Rossi put a restraining hand on his son's shoulder. "Come on. You just need to develop your coordination."

"I'm trying to," Jonathan said stubbornly.

"All right. We'll just keep trying harder."

Jonathan didn't understand about this "we" business. He was the one who had to get out on the courts and make a fool of himself whenever the Wildcats had a game.

Jonathan tossed and turned that night and finally decided he needed to give himself a pep talk. Negativity was deadly to athletes. So, in his mind, he went over his playing at the community center last year. He had made baskets, and of course, he had been the captain of the team. He fell asleep counting the points he had made.

By Monday's practice, Jonathan had talked himself into feeling better about basketball in general and himself in particular. Maybe he was just in a slump. Even the best players went through that, and they always came out of it. At least he had never heard of a player who hadn't.

"Hey, who's that?" Paul asked as they left the locker room dressed and ready to practice.

Jonathan looked around and then spotted the person Paul meant. A tall lanky kid stood talking to Coach Davidson. Though deep in conversation, the boy bounced a basketball with his right hand.

Mike joined them. "His name is Billy Page. He just came to Mr. Jacobs's class this morning."

Jonathan stared thoughtfully at Billy. "Ham said some new kid was going to be on the team. This must be the guy. He was a star at his old school."

"He doesn't look so hot." Mike sniffed.

"He looks tall," Paul said, giving Billy the

once-over. "He's about as tall as two of the fifth graders put together."

Mike gave him a poke. "Funny, Paul. Anyway, if he's that good, he can take Ham's place at guard."

Really tall players didn't usually play guard, Jonathan thought. They were usually forwards, like Mike. Or centers, like him.

Coach Davidson blew on his whistle. "Line up, everyone." Whatever troubles they had on the court, by this time the team knew how to line up to the coach's satisfaction.

He motioned Billy to come and stand next to him, giving Jonathan plenty of time to observe his new teammate. If there was one word to sum up Billy Page, it was confident. Jonathan knew he would have hated standing in front of a bunch of strange guys. Billy looked pleased, as if they had all assembled just to meet him.

"This is your new teammate," Coach Davidson said, his hand on Billy's shoulder. "His name is Billy Page, and he played center at his school in Oakville."

Center, darn, Jonathan thought. Why did he have to play center?

"So let's have a practice game now."

As Jonathan feared, Billy went in as center. Jonathan was now playing forward.

It was the hardest practice session the Wildcats had ever had. The coach barked out orders, and the boys attempted to follow them. Even Jonathan had to admit Billy made the rest of the team look good, but that was because he seemed to be everywhere on the court. If someone passed him the ball, he caught it. He stuffed the ball through the basket on rebounds. As Jonathan huffed and puffed down the court, he caught sight of Coach Davidson, whose face was bright as sunshine in the morning.

Finally, the coach blew on his whistle once more. "Good," he said. Coming from Coach Davidson, that was pretty high praise. Then he added surprisingly, "There won't be any practice Wednesday."

Jonathan and Mike exchanged looks. What could be serious enough for the coach to call off one of his beloved practice sessions?

"The gym floor is being washed and waxed," Coach Davidson said curtly. "We'll reschedule to Thursday and have our regular practice on Friday. You may go."

Usually, the boys stampeded out of the gym,

but today they were so tired that they walked out in slow motion.

"Do you think we should say something to him?" Mike asked, pointing in Billy's direction.

Jonathan wasn't feeling very charitable toward Billy, but he shrugged and nodded. "I guess."

Mike walked over to the locker where Billy was peeling off his T-shirt. "Hi," he said gruffly. "I'm Mike Stone."

"And I'm Jonathan Rossi," Jonathan said, joining them.

Billy looked them over coolly. "Hi."

"You looked pretty good out there," Mike said.

"You didn't," Billy said bluntly.

Jonathan bristled at Billy's words. "We haven't been playing that long."

"Well, if this team is going to make anything happen, it had better start. There're only about ten games in the whole season. And you've already lost two."

"Thanks for reminding us," Mike said sarcastically.

Billy threw his shirt into the locker and grabbed a towel from his gym bag. "Don't worry, I'll help you."

Mike made a face. "Boy, I thought big stars were supposed to be humble."

Though Jonathan admired Mike's courage, he didn't feel like getting into a fight with someone he hardly knew. "Come on," he said, poking Mike in the back. "Let's get out of here."

"Sure. Billy probably has a dinner date with the Bulls. We wouldn't want him to be late."

Billy didn't even look mad. He just gave them a condescending smile and headed for the shower.

When he disappeared, Mike said angrily, "That guy has some nerve. He acts like he's the only guy in the world who knows how to dunk a basketball."

Jonathan sighed. "Well, maybe not in the world, but he might be the only guy on the Wildcats."

C H A P T E R
EIGHT

Ham took a bite of his tuna sandwich. "Anybody want to trade?" he asked, making a face.

"You're not much of a salesman, Ham," Bobby Glickman remarked.

"Would you buy a used tuna sandwich from this guy?" Jonathan joked.

Ham ignored all the teasing comments. "I'm going back into the line to buy a hamburger." He rose, felt around in his pockets, and then sat back down. "I don't have enough money."

"What was all that jingling I heard?" Bobby asked.

"Yeah," Jonathan chimed in. "It sounds like you emptied your piggy bank in there."

"I need that money for a haircut," Ham said

disgustedly. "I have to get one for the dance." Ham had gotten tired of waiting for Veronica to make a decision, and he had asked Sharon.

"But the dance isn't until the Saturday after Christmas break," Jonathan said.

Ham sat back down and started picking pieces of bread off of his sandwich. "Well, you know how Mr. Fenn cuts hair."

"Yeah," Bobby said gloomily. "Too short."

"So, if I want it to look even halfway decent, I have to get it cut today."

Jonathan swallowed a sip of milk. "I'm glad my mother lets me go to the guy who cuts her hair. Fenn's barbershop gives me the creeps."

Ham sat up a little straighter. It was apparent he could make fun of his barbershop but he didn't like anyone else to. "Well, at least it's a man's place," he said. "There's not a bunch of ladies in rollers sitting around yapping."

"The Clip Joint happens to be a unisex shop," Jonathan responded indignantly.

"Oh, come on," Bobby said, "don't tell me you guys are going to fight about your beauty shops." He dragged the word *beauty* out about three syllables.

Now both Ham and Jonathan started to laugh. "I guess not," Jonathan said.

"But I still say Fenn's barbershop is a man's

place," Ham insisted. "You guys should come with me after school." He lowered his voice to a confidential whisper. "He's got dirty magazines."

Now Bobby spoke up. "I've gotten a couple of haircuts at Fenn's. Ham's right. I've seen 'em. *Playboy, Penthouse,* he's got all of them."

"Do you get to look at them while you're there?" Jonathan asked excitedly. The only magazines lying around the Clip Joint were *Glamour* and *Ladies' Home Journal.*

Ham and Bobby exchanged looks. "Well," Ham began, "old man Fenn doesn't let kids read those magazines. Actually, there's a sign up that says, ADULT LITERATURE FOR THOSE OVER EIGHTEEN."

Jonathan leaned back in his seat. "So, it's no big deal. Why should we go to the barbershop with you?"

Ham leaned forward and motioned his friends to come closer. "I heard about a guy who stole some of those magazines from Fenn's."

Jonathan perked up. Now, that was an interesting idea. His father never had those kinds of magazines at home, and he was curious about them. "I'd like to look over a couple of copies," he conceded.

130

"And while you're keeping Mr. Fenn busy with your haircut, we nab the magazines, right, Ham?" Bobby looked excited.

"That's it, Bobby. It would be easy. Of course, we'd take them back," Ham added virtuously. "Someday."

"And the gym floor is being washed. I don't even have practice after school," Jonathan mused. It seemed like an omen.

"Well then?" Ham asked.

"It's okay by me," Bobby said.

"Me, too," Jonathan added.

"Great." Ham broke into a wide smile. "But there is one thing."

"What's that?" Bobby demanded.

"I really can't expect to accomplish this mission on an empty stomach." He looked down at his tuna sandwich, now torn into disgusting little pieces.

"Oh, here." Jonathan threw half a peanut butter and jelly sandwich, which Ham caught more deftly than he ever had a basketball.

"And you can have my apple," Bobby said, handing it over.

"What? No cookies?" Noting Bobby and Jonathan's hostile glares, he hastily said, "That's all right. This should hold me."

It was hard for Jonathan to keep his mind on

his work for the rest of the afternoon. He began to wonder whether he was some kind of a pervert.

Once David had brought one of those magazines home, and his mother had found it hidden under his bed when she changed the sheets. David had accused her of spying, but his mother had pointed out that if David changed his own sheets—as he was supposed to—she never would have found it. Then David had tried a different tack. He told his parents he had decided to become an artist and had heard they had to know how to draw nude bodies. That hadn't worked, either. His father had thrown out the magazine and told David he could start his art career by drawing bowls of fruit.

"Jonathan, why are you just staring out the window like that?"

Jonathan jerked back into the present. Robin was staring down at him.

"It's time for art," she continued.

Mrs. Volini's class went upstairs to the studio for art class. Jonathan shoved his books in his desk and followed Robin to the door.

"Have you decided what you are going to do for your art project?" Robin said.

Jonathan's mind had been on the human

form, but he didn't think his teacher would appreciate his renderings of that subject. "I guess I'll make a fort out of toothpicks," he said finally. It would be easy to call his mom after school and tell her he needed to stop downtown and buy some toothpicks and glue.

"Remind me, I have to stop at the store and pick up some things for art," Jonathan told Ham as they waited for Bobby to show up outside the school entrance.

"Is that your alibi?"

"It's not an alibi," Jonathan said indignantly. "Not exactly."

Bobby came running up to them. "Sorry I'm late."

"Where were you?" Ham asked irritably. "My mother told me Mr. Fenn wanted me there no later than three o'clock."

"Since when do you have to make an appointment with a barber?" Jonathan hooted.

"Can I help it if he's a popular barber?" He turned to Bobby. "So where were you?"

"Asking Jessica to the dance."

Jonathan figured Bobby had asked Jessica because she was one of the shortest girls in the sixth grade.

They discussed the dance all the way downtown. It was a way to keep their minds off the caper they were about to pull, but finally Jonathan asked, "Do we have the plan down?"

"It's not much of a plan," Ham said. "I get Mr. Fenn interested in cutting my hair, and you guys try and stuff some magazines into your backpacks."

"I think it'll work," Bobby said cheerfully. In his usual confident way, he marched into Fenn's barbershop.

Fenn's barbershop sure looked different from the Clip Joint, Jonathan thought to himself. Instead of a large mirrored room, full of stylists cutting and blow-drying hair, the small shop contained only two worn leather barber chairs facing a round cracked mirror. In front of the small picture window was a round coffee table covered with magazines and surrounded by a few low benches. Jonathan tried to catch some of the magazine titles out of the corner of his eye, but the only one he saw was *Popular Mechanics*.

Mr. Fenn, thin and dour, stood behind the far chair, snipping the hair of an elderly man who didn't have much to begin with. He frowned when he saw the trio. "Kevin Berger?"

"Yes, Mr. Fenn?"

"Are these boys getting haircuts?"

"Not exactly, Mr. Fenn."

"They are either getting haircuts or they are not. Since they don't have appointments, I assume they are not."

"We were just going to wait for Ham, I mean Kevin." Bobby smiled. It was the same smile he used in the commercial where he was trying to persuade his dad to buy a certain kind of fried chicken.

Mr. Fenn pointed to a sign above the mirror, so old its faded edges were curling up. "No loitering," Mr. Fenn said, as though they couldn't read.

"But we're not loitering," Bobby said. "We're waiting. Besides, it's cold out." Bobby rubbed his arms up and down as though he was freezing. Actually, it was pretty warm outside. Jonathan admired Bobby's courage in taking on Mr. Fenn, but he felt the overacting wasn't helping their cause.

Mr. Fenn didn't seem impressed, either. Before he could banish them, however, the customer turned his head slightly, looked them over, and then said, "C'mon, Fenn. Don't be such a meany. Let the boys sit a spell."

Jonathan and Bobby stood in the doorway looking positively angelic.

"Aw, sit down," Mr. Fenn said, moving his clippers in the general direction of the benches.

Jonathan felt both relieved and guilty as he took a seat. Bobby looked longingly at the magazines, but Jonathan shook his head at him. It would be better to wait until Mr. Fenn was fully involved with Ham's hair before making a move.

After the man paid and left, with a tip of his hat to the boys, Ham took his place in the barber's chair. Mr. Fenn cranked the seat up so that Ham was at the proper height.

"So what do you want today, Kevin?" Mr. Fenn asked.

Ham shrugged. "A haircut."

Jonathan and Bobby snickered in the background.

"Yes, Kevin, that's why I'm here all day . . . to give people haircuts," Mr. Fenn said drily. "Anything special you want me to do with it?"

"Just don't make it too short," Ham pleaded.

Mr. Fenn started attacking Ham's hair with the clippers. "I never make it too short."

The loud buzz of the clippers made it hard for Ham to keep up lively conversation, but he made the effort. "So what do you think of the

Bears' chances of getting to the Super Bowl?" he began bravely.

Meanwhile, Jonathan and Bobby were doing their best to paw unobtrusively through the magazines. The good ones all seemed to be buried at the bottom of the pile.

When Mr. Fenn glanced in his direction, Jonathan made a big deal of taking his large geography book out of his backpack. He held it up as if to say, Look at what a good student I am, studying in the barbershop. As soon as Mr. Fenn returned to Ham, Jonathan once more began moving the magazines around, trying to find one with a woman on the cover.

Bobby, with his back to Mr. Fenn, had a better opportunity to search. Jonathan watched as Bobby looked under all the many men's fashion magazines thrown casually on top of the heap. When he gave a low whistle under his breath, Jonathan knew he had struck pay dirt.

Bobby inched the magazine out of the pile. He was about to show it to Jonathan when the doorbell jingled and another customer entered the store.

"Well, hello there."

Jonathan would have known that voice anywhere, even though it was usually saying "You call that a dribble?"

"Hello, Coach Davidson." Jonathan gulped. He watched as Bobby quickly shoved the magazine back into the pile. A good half of the cover still stuck out, though.

Coach Davidson settled himself next to Bobby, who gave him a friendly smile. "Hi, Coach."

Mr. Davidson nodded at him absently. Although he had Bobby in gym class, obviously he hadn't made much of an impression.

"So, Rossi, I see we're using our day away from practice for the same purpose," Coach Davidson said.

For one wild moment, Jonathan thought Coach Davidson meant he was here to steal dirty magazines, too. Then, Jonathan realized there was only one reason to be sitting in Fenn's barbershop.

"I'm not having a haircut. I'm waiting for Ham," Jonathan said.

Coach Davidson glanced over to the chair where Ham was looking nervously into the mirror, watching the whole scene out of the corner of his eye.

"I see."

An uncomfortable silence settled over the

group. Jonathan racked his brain for something to talk about—something other than basketball. Nothing came to mind. Finally, Bobby, taking a leaf from Ham's book, asked. "Do you think the Bears are going to the Super Bowl, sir?"

Even Mr. Davidson looked relieved that some sort of a topic had come up. Like a good athlete, he took the ball and ran with it, launching into a five-minute discourse of the strengths and weaknesses of the Chicago Bears.

Jonathan tried to act as if he was hanging on the coach's every word. Actually, it was hard to keep his eyes away from Bobby's magazine, which pulled at him like a magnet.

"I'm finished." A newly shorn Ham was standing at Jonathan's shoulder.

Coach Davidson looked Ham over coolly. "Hello, Kevin."

"Hi. Well, we have to be going, don't we, guys?" Ham said nervously. He shook his head at Jonathan and Bobby as if to say, Don't you dare try it. Not with Davidson here.

Jonathan glanced longingly at the magazine. He supposed it wouldn't be such a big deal if he had to leave it, but what a waste of an afternoon.

Coach Davidson got up and moved to where Mr. Fenn was waiting, clippers at the ready.

Then he turned back to Jonathan. "Rossi, I want to see some improvement from you in practice tomorrow."

Jonathan cringed. Why did Davidson have to bring that up now?

"Now that we have Page, I want the rest of you guys to start showing me something. Maybe we can get some kind of team going."

"Right." Jonathan stuffed his geography book into his book bag.

"What's the matter?" Mr. Fenn asked. "Your basketball team's no good?"

"Let's just say some of the boys have their problems," Mr. Davidson said as he settled himself into the chair.

"Practice. Practice makes perfect," Mr. Fenn quoted as he ran a comb through Coach Davidson's thick blond locks.

"You've got it," the coach agreed.

"Come on, let's get out of here," Jonathan hissed. He certainly didn't need to stand around and listen to a barber telling him how to play basketball.

"Ah . . . bye," Ham said as he threw on his coat.

Jonathan gave a halfhearted wave and followed Bobby out the door.

"Boy, what a big nothing that turned out to

be," Jonathan said as soon as the door slammed shut behind him.

"I'm sorry," Ham replied. "Who knew that Davidson was going to show up?"

"Really. I get one afternoon away from that guy—"

"I wouldn't say it was a big nothing," Bobby broke in, a sly smile on his face.

"What do you mean?" Ham asked.

Bobby patted the book bag that was slung over his shoulder. "You'll see."

Jonathan and Ham exchanged wide-eyed looks. "When?" Ham asked excitedly. "When did you get it?"

"And how?" Jonathan demanded.

Bobby motioned them away from the barbershop and into the alley a few doors down.

"It was when Davidson and Mr. Fenn were talking about practicing. I decided to practice lifting magazines."

Ham slapped his head in disbelief. "I don't believe it. They could have looked at you at any second. You would have been caught by a barber *and* a teacher."

"But they didn't catch me," Bobby pointed out sensibly. "Besides, they were so busy talking to each other, I knew they wouldn't look in my direction."

Jonathan was full of admiration for Bobby. He was really gutsy. "So let's see it," he demanded.

Bobby was about to pull the magazine from his book bag when a lady with a shopping bag entered the alley. She looked at the boys curiously as she passed by.

"This isn't safe," Bobby said.

"So where do we go?" Jonathan asked.

Ham looked at his watch. "I have to go home."

"Can you keep the magazine at your house, Jon?" Bobby asked.

Jonathan shook his head. "My brother tried that once. My folks weren't too happy when they found it."

"Don't look at me," Ham said. "I share a room with a nosy little brother."

"Well, I can't keep it, either," Bobby said flatly. "My mom gets mad if I have comic books in the house."

"Then what do we do with it?" Jonathan asked.

The trio looked at each other glumly. Then Ham got excited. "Wait, I know."

"What?"

"There's an empty lot a block away from my

142

house. I can bury it there, and we can come back later and read it."

Jonathan slapped Ham on the back. "Now you're thinking."

"It should work," Bobby agreed. He pulled the magazine from his book bag. Ham and Jonathan clamored to have a look, but Bobby held it over his head. "Hey, this is for all of us to read together." He glanced around the alley. "Besides, we decided this isn't a good place to hang around."

"All right, all right," Ham grumbled. He turned so his backpack was facing Bobby. "Just put it in here."

Bobby stuffed it in the sack. "And don't look when you bury it."

"By the time I get to the empty lot, it will be dark. I won't be able to look at it even if I wanted to."

"And don't forget where you bury it," Jonathan admonished him.

Ham got a pained expression on his face. "Boy, what do you think I am, some kind of dork?"

Bobby just shook his head, while Jonathan said, "Don't make me answer that, Ham."

CHAPTER
NINE

Jonathan walked into the house and threw his backpack into the hall closet.

"Hi, Jon," his mother called from the kitchen, where she had her schoolbooks spread out over the table.

He joined her in the kitchen, opened the refrigerator, and pulled out a quart of milk. His first inclination was to gulp some right out of the carton, but he knew that wasn't a good idea with his mother looking at him. He went to the cupboard and got a glass.

"Did you get your toothpicks?" Mrs. Rossi asked as she made some notes on a pad of paper.

The toothpicks. "No."

Mrs. Rossi glanced up at him with surprise. "Why not?"

Jonathan had had enough of subterfuge for one day. "I was hanging around with Ham and Bobby Glickman, and I forgot."

"Oh, Jon." His mother sighed.

"Sorry, Mom." Though he wasn't exactly sure for which of his misdeeds he was apologizing.

"Your dad's home," she informed him, going back to her work.

Jonathan glanced at the clock. "So early?"

"Yes, his last appointment canceled. Why don't you go say hi to him? He's in the den."

Jonathan grabbed his milk and headed into the large comfortable room. He expected to see his father watching the news as he usually did when he got home in time for it. Instead, his father was sprawled on the floor thumbing through the record albums that occupied a long shelf in the bookcase.

"Dad, what are you doing?"

"Oh, hi, Jon," his father said without looking up. "I'm looking for a record.

Jonathan went over and sat down beside him. "What record?"

"It's by the Mamas and the Papas. I know I had it once," he muttered to himself.

"The Mamas and the Papas." Jonathan laughed.

Mr. Rossi looked up. "I suppose all the groups you like have sensible names," he said, but he was smiling. "Here it is." He pulled out a dog-eared album jacket. "I heard one of their songs on the oldies station coming home and I wanted to hear a few more cuts from the album."

"That album looks like it's been around for a long time."

"Yeah. I bought it in college." Mr. Rossi frowned. "Or was it high school?"

"It's probably pretty scratchy."

Mr. Rossi drew the record out of its sleeve. Even from where Jonathan was sitting, he could see marks on it.

"I never did take very good care of my records. Maybe I'll buy another one."

"They hardly make albums anymore, Dad. Now it's compact discs."

"Yes, Jonathan, I've heard about compact discs. I'm not that out of it."

"It's just that I never see you listening to records."

"I used to," Mr. Rossi said, looking down at the battered album jacket. "I used to listen to them all the time."

"What happened?"

"I guess I've just been too busy lately."

Jonathan could understand being too busy for the things you liked to do.

Mr. Rossi refocused on his son. "So how was practice today?"

Jonathan immediately felt a red flush spreading from his neck to his face, but he merely said, "It was canceled. The gym floor was being washed."

"Can't they do that on Saturday?"

Jonathan got up. "I'm going to go study."

"I've been meaning to ask you something. Didn't you tell me a new kid was coming to play after Thanksgiving?"

"Billy Page," Jonathan said reluctantly.

"So how is he?"

"He's going to be a big addition." Maybe too big, Jonathan thought to himself. Before his dad could question him further, Jonathan went upstairs.

Jonathan thought he might get started on his project about advertising. As part of their unit on "Truth or Consequences," each member of the class was supposed to choose five television commercials and pick out the points that seemed honest and those that didn't. This was one of the best assignments Jonathan ever had, giving him a valid excuse to watch unlimited amounts of television. His parents had even allowed him to put their portable black and white TV in his room for the length of his project. Before he settled in, David called him into his room.

"Hey, Jon, can you loan me five dollars?"

"Five dollars! I just loaned you two dollars a couple of weeks ago, which you never paid back."

David tipped back in his desk chair. Jonathan was afraid he was going to fall over, but he balanced himself like an acrobat on a tightrope. "I want to buy somebody a Christmas present."

"Oh . . . somebody. Let's see, 'somebody' wouldn't be Mom or Dad. And even you're not crude enough to borrow money from me for my present." He pointed his forefinger at David. "I'm guessing that it must be Amanda."

David waved a casual hand. "So what if it is, Sherlock?"

"Well, I'm sorry. I've got to save money for Robin's present." Then he wondered whether that was true. Was he actually going to buy Robin a gift?

"You and Robin are really tight, then?" David tipped his chair back into place. He leered at Jonathan. "Just how tight are you?"

"Oh, David, you're gross." Jonathan turned to walk out of the room.

"Hey, hey, don't go so fast. I'm your big brother. I want to help you."

"With what?" Jonathan asked suspiciously.

"I don't know. With whatever you need. Take this dance, for instance. You ready for it?"

Jonathan sat down on David's bed. "I don't know. I just show up, don't I?"

"Yeah, you show up." David rose and started pacing. "But how do you get there?"

"I guess Mom or Dad will drive us."

"You want to go with them?"

"David, last I heard, eleven-year-olds can't get licenses. Neither can fourteen-year-olds, or I'd ask you to take us."

"Look, all I'm trying to tell you is you don't want either of your parents in the driver's seat. It's too embarrassing. Mom will keep smiling at Robin and asking her all kinds of personal questions, and Dad will be worse. He won't say anything."

Now Jonathan began to worry. David had a point. "So how do I get to the dance?" he asked anxiously. "Have Robin's parents take us?"

"No, that would be terrible. Then her mother will start asking *you* questions."

"So what's the answer?"

"Double with someone and let his parents drive," David said triumphantly. "Then if his parents start acting up, you won't be the one who's humiliated."

Jonathan looked at David with admiration. Maybe it was a good idea that David take an interest in his affairs. He never would have thought this driving angle out for himself. "Okay, what else will I need to know?" Jonathan asked.

David looked up thoughtfully at the ceiling. "What about corsages?"

"I'm all right on that one," Jonathan said, relieved that he had a handle on something. "The girls decided they weren't going to wear them."

"Well, they could change their minds, but let's take their word on it for the moment." He whirled around. "Can you dance?"

"Dance? I guess so."

"Have you ever danced?"

Jonathan thought about it. He had been to a couple of birthday parties where the boys and girls had danced together. Actually, that wasn't quite true. The boys had stood in the corner, having a contest to see who could eat the most sandwiches, while the girls had danced with each other. It hadn't looked that hard, though.

David looked at him with pity. "You don't know until you try. You may be lousy."

Jonathan nervously rubbed his hands together. He hadn't thought about being a lousy dancer. He assumed you just got on the dance floor and moved around. "So where do I learn to dance?" he asked.

"I don't know." David shrugged.

"Well that's just great, David. First you tell me I'm going to stink up the dance floor, but you don't give me any ideas about how I can learn. Who taught you?"

An embarrassed frown crossed David's face. "Mom."

"Mom? You danced with Mom?" Jonathan hooted.

"Yes." David's frown turned into a scowl. "And big help she was. She taught me something called the fox-trot, which they haven't danced in about fifty years. And the fast dances, forget it."

Jonathan ran his hands through his hair. "So who should I get to teach me?"

"Why not ask Robin?"

"Robin? I don't want her to know that I can't dance."

"She's going to find out soon enough."

Jonathan considered this. "I guess you're right. I could ask her to teach me."

"Sure, she'll be glad to," David said encouragingly. "After all, she doesn't want you stepping all over her."

"Okay. I'll ask her."

Jonathan got up. "Thanks for the advice."

David put his arm out to stop him. "Pretty valuable advice."

"What do you mean?"

"I just saved you from looking stupid about three different ways."

"So?"

"So I think you should pay for that advice. It has to be worth at least five dollars."

Jonathan kicked himself for not seeing this coming. "I told you I need it myself."

"Hey, you're the moneybags in this family. You could loan me five dollars and not even miss it."

"I don't want to. You still owe me two dollars, anyway."

David shrugged. "Gee, then I'll just have to mention to Mom that you need a few dancing lessons. And maybe I'll remind Dad you need a ride to the dance."

"You wouldn't!" Jonathan exploded.

David's expression turned regretful. "I may have to if you don't pay me what's rightfully mine. I think I earned the five dollars."

Jonathan knew when he was licked. "All right, all right, but it's a loan."

"I wouldn't have it any other way."

Jonathan slammed out of David's room. Booby-trapped again. He flung himself on his bed. At least this time he had gotten something for his money. Usually, David just cheated him out of it. He began to think about dancing with Robin. He looked pretty graceful, moving like Michael Jackson. Then another picture popped up. There he was running awkwardly down the court. Jonathan sighed. If only Robin could teach him to dribble.

Jonathan asked Robin about the dancing lessons the next day at lunch; putting it off would have been worse agony. He pulled her aside after she dumped her leftovers into the round metal container at the back of the lunchroom, and then glanced furtively around. "Could you teach me how to dance?" He blurted it out.

"Sure," Robin said.

Jonathan admired her for acting as if dancing lessons were no big deal.

"When do you want to do it?" Robin asked.

"How about tomorrow?"

"I thought you had practice on Fridays." She gave him a funny look. "Wouldn't you rather do it on the weekend?"

Jonathan hadn't picked Friday lightly. He had practice this afternoon because of yesterday's cancellation, and the thought of getting out on the court two days in a row was really a bummer. So what if I miss a practice for a change? he thought belligerently. I deserve a day off. "Let's just make it tomorrow," he said.

Robin shrugged. "If that's what you want."

Although he felt a little guilty about skipping Friday practice, Jonathan was glad he was going to be missing a day as he watched Billy on the court that afternoon. Jonathan was tall, but Billy was tall and agile. When Billy made a jump shot—from the top of his jump—the ball flew into the basket. Jonathan was stabbed by jealousy. He looked over at Mike to see whether he was feeling the same way, but Mike, dribbling the ball down the court, seemed more focused and intent than ever.

He wanted to talk to Mike about it, but when he tried to catch up with him after practice, Mike was walking out of the locker room with Billy. He almost went up to them, then he turned back. Slowly, Jonathan drew on his jacket and then made sure his backpack was securely in place. When he was almost positive that Mike and Billy were gone, he headed out into the corridor.

"Hello, Jonathan," a voice behind him called. Coach Brown was moving slowly down the hall, supported by crutches.

"Coach Brown!" His eyes moved down to the coach's leg. "You're still in a cast," he said with disappointment.

"Back in a cast," the coach corrected. "I was out of it for a few days. Then they found out the pins the doctors put in my leg weren't holding, so they had to go in and fix them." He made a face. "And the doctors think I'm going to need a little more repair work."

Jonathan didn't know what to say. Finally, he choked out, "So that means you won't be coming back for a while."

"Not until spring, anyway. I'm on leave of absence."

Jonathan hadn't realized how much he missed the coach until right now.

Coach Brown motioned to a bench outside the principal's office. "It's hard for me to stand, Jon. Why don't we sit down for a minute and you can tell me how the Wildcats are doing."

Jonathan dutifully followed the coach over to the bench.

"You've got a big game coming up with the Blue Point Rams."

"Yeah. We lost our first two games."

"You'll improve. I hear Coach Davidson is really working you hard."

"He sure is," Jonathan said glumly.

"What's wrong, Jon?" the coach asked.

Normally, Jonathan would have said, "Nothing," but there was something about the way the coach was looking at him that made Jonathan feel as if the tight knot that was usually in his chest these days was loosening a little.

"I guess I don't like playing as much as I thought I would," he said quietly.

The coach raised his eyebrows.

Jonathan leaned his head back against the wall, avoiding the coach's eyes. "I'm not too good."

"Now that surprises me."

Jonathan's voice took on more color. "We

practice too much. And Coach Davidson keeps trying to motivate us by telling us we're lousy."

Once Jonathan began his litany of reasons for disliking basketball, he couldn't seem to stop. On he went, talking about how he didn't have time to do other things, and how bad he felt about Ham leaving the team. He spent several moments discussing the talents of Billy Page.

"Well," the coach said when Jonathan finally stopped to take a breath, "if you feel that strongly about things, Jon, why don't you quit?"

Jonathan swiveled toward him. "I couldn't do that," he said in a shocked voice.

Coach Brown shrugged. "They haven't signed you to a contract, have they?"

"Hardly." Jonathan once again stared at the wall.

"All I can say, Jon, is that life's too short to spend time doing things you don't like. Sometimes you have to. I mean, you just can't give up on math if you don't take a shine to it, for instance. But plenty of things are optional and sports is one of them. Maybe you'll decide to play next year, or in high school. Maybe you won't. It's up to you."

Jonathan felt confusion rolling over him.

There was no way he could quit the basketball team. He didn't understand how the coach could think there was. "Well, I'll probably stick with it," he muttered.

The coach got unsteadily to his feet. "If that's what you want. I won't even tell you to work hard. I know you're doing that. But at least try to have fun with the game. That's what it's all about."

Jonathan walked Coach Brown to the parking lot and then headed toward home. He was glad that the coach understood his situation. At least somebody did. Sighing, he thought about Billy Page and the way he so lightly handled the basketball, as if it was a soap bubble that would break if you touched it. Maybe one day he'd be able to handle the ball like that. He could work toward that goal, anyway.

But have fun with the game, like Coach Brown said? That he doubted. In fact, he couldn't think of anything that was less fun at the moment than playing basketball.

C H A P T E R
TEN

Jonathan had hoped he could avoid his team-mates and sneak out after school on Friday for his dance lesson at Robin's house. First, though, he had to make a stop at the "lost and found" to see whether someone had turned in his new sweater, which he vaguely remembered leaving on the playground. He told Robin she might as well go home, and he'd take the second bus to her place.

He was relieved to see his sweater in the lost and found box, though it was now slightly soiled, as if someone had stepped on it. Stuffing it into his book bag, he was heading for the bus when he saw Mike Stone coming down the hall. Jonathan ducked into the bathroom.

After giving Mike plenty of time to pass by, he slipped out again, only to bump into Billy Page heading for the gym.

"Hey, Rossi, you're going the wrong way."

"Oh, I'm not going to practice today." Jonathan gave him a bright, fake smile.

"Why not?"

He waited too long before finally saying, "I've got an appointment."

Billy looked at him steadily. "You're not blowing off practice are you?"

"Look, I'm going to be late," Jonathan said, trying to walk around Billy.

"You're not that bad, Rossi."

Jonathan didn't know whether to be pleased or insulted. Finally, he said, "It's just one practice."

"Sure." Billy adjusted his gym bag on his shoulder. "I'll see you Monday."

That Page had a lot of nerve. Jonathan had been to every practice session and where had it gotten him? He slammed out the front door into the school yard. The cool air felt good on his face. It was still unseasonably warm for a Midwest winter, great weather in fact. He tried not to think of how many afternoons he had missed by being in that overheated, sweaty-smelling gym.

He rode the second bus over to Robin's house, trying to think up an excuse to give Coach Davidson if he asked about his whereabouts. He didn't want to lie if he didn't have to. Finally, he decided he would say he had spent the afternoon helping a friend. This was almost true. By learning how to dance, he was helping Robin avoid a bad time at the dance.

When Jonathan arrived at Robin's door, she whisked him inside with barely a hello. "We're going up to my bedroom," she said curtly.

"Your bedroom?" Jonathan squeaked. Then he could have kicked himself. Why didn't he act as though he was invited up to girls' bedrooms every day of the week?

"My mother is having some friends over and needs to use the living room. She's picking up one of them now. She wasn't very happy about it, but she said we could come up here if we . . ." Robin's face turned bright pink. "Never mind."

"Well, what did she think we were going to do?" Jonathan muttered.

"Here we are," Robin said, flinging the door open. Jonathan had never seen such a clean room in his life. The white furniture all looked as if it had been purchased yesterday, and Robin's room was free from clutter. Even her books were stacked neatly on her desk.

"This is neat."

"Thank you," Robin said. Then she peered at him. "Or do you mean tidy?"

"It's both," Jonathan said diplomatically, although tidy was what he had been thinking.

Now that Jonathan was actually standing in her room, waiting to dance, it was clear that Robin was a little unnerved by the prospect of getting started. "Why don't we pick out some music," Robin said.

"That's the record player?" Jonathan asked, pointing to a child's small record player sitting on Robin's dresser.

"The stereo is in the living room," Robin replied crossly. "And my tape deck is in the shop. This plays all right."

Jonathan held up his hands. "I believe you."

Robin walked over to the stack of records leaning against the dresser. "I think we should start with something fast."

"Fine," a relieved Jonathan answered. He wasn't very eager to put his arms around Robin right off the bat.

Robin pulled out two records. "What do you think of these?"

"Put on the Dennis Brothers," Jonathan requested. He rubbed his moist hands against his jeans.

The music began blaring through the room, and Robin quickly turned down the volume. "Oops, a little too loud."

They stood across the room, just looking at each other for what seemed like an hour to Jonathan. At last, Robin crossed to the empty space in the middle of the floor and said, "Well you just go like this."

Jonathan watched in fascination as Robin began bumping and rolling in time to the music. Her hips went one way, her arms and head another. Her feet didn't do much at all, except for the little prancing steps she made as she swayed. "There," she said when the song ended. "You got it?"

Jonathan suspected he did not. "Now which way did your arms go?"

"I'm not sure," Robin said, wrinkling her brow. "You just kind of move with the music."

"Oh, right," Jonathan mumbled.

Robin put her hands on Jonathan's arms in a businesslike manner and tried to adjust them into the right position. The next song was already drumming away. "All right, move."

Jonathan moved. He wasn't sure he was moving correctly, or even why he was gyrating the way he was, but he did wiggle around in time to the music.

"Great," Robin said, clapping her hands.

Jonathan stopped dancing. "You're kidding, right?"

"I am not. You're just naturally graceful."

When Jonathan's disbelieving look did not disappear, she turned him around so he was facing the mirror on the back of her closet door. "Now dance," she instructed.

With fascination, Jonathan watched his reflection in the mirror. A smile creased his face for the first time since he had walked in Robin's door. He could dance. He added a few flourishes to the steps he was already doing. Michael Jackson had nothing on him.

Robin joined him, and they shimmied and gyrated through two more songs. When they were done, Jonathan collapsed on Robin's bed. "Boy, I'm more tired than I am after a basketball game."

Robin hovered at the foot of the bed. "We'll take a break and then we'll try slow dancing."

She looked at the empty space on her bed next to Jonathan's sprawled body and then she sat on the floor.

Feeling a little uncomfortable about the way he had taken over Robin's bed, Jonathan sat up, wishing he had a handkerchief. He was afraid he had just wiped his sweat all over Robin's bedspread. He reached over and picked up a book from the stack sitting on her desk. Then he realized it was one of the Battle of the Books selections. He put it back guiltily. To avoid Robin's asking him just how far along he was with his reading, Jonathan asked, "Have you come up with any ideas for your moral dilemma?"

"I thought I might write about Veronica turning all the girls against me. I had a chance to do the same thing to her, but I didn't."

"That's a good one."

"What about you?" Robin asked. Before Jonathan could answer, Mrs. Miller appeared in the doorway.

"Knock, knock," she said as she stuck her head in the room. She took in Jonathan on the bed and Robin on the floor with a glance. "I thought you two were supposed to be dancing."

"We were," Robin replied in an exasperated tone. "We're just resting."

"All right. I'll be downstairs with my company if you need anything." She opened the door a little wider before disappearing.

Jonathan checked his watch. "I suppose we should finish the dancing lesson. I have to call my mom so she can pick me up before five."

Robin got up and started flipping through her records. "Do you want to keep doing fast dancing?"

"We haven't tried anything slow." While Robin's back was turned, he breathed quickly into his cupped hands. David said that was a sure way to see whether your breath was bad. Even though he had only had a hamburger and fries for lunch, he didn't want to take a chance on getting close to her with bad breath. It seemed okay.

Robin picked out a record and put it on the player. It was a song Jonathan didn't recognize, but it was dreamy and soft. Robin stood in the middle of the floor, waiting, so Jonathan, feeling as if he was going before a firing squad, got up and went over to her.

"Put your arm around my waist," Robin said, her voice barely audible.

Jonathan did as he was told. Then he grasped Robin's hand, wishing he'd had the foresight to wipe his hands again. "Now what?" he asked gruffly.

"Now we dance."

Jonathan wasn't sure you could call what they did dancing. He shuffled back and forth, kind of pulling Robin along with him. He had to concentrate on so many things. Number one was keeping his feet out from under Robin's. Sometimes they seemed to get dangerously close. He also made sure his mouth was closed, just in case there was some bad breath lurking, waiting to pop out. His arm stayed loosely around her waist. Too tight, and she might think he was some kind of sex pervert.

Then Jonathan had a horrible thought. He had a small mole next to his ear. Normally, it wasn't noticeable, but no one had ever been quite so close to his ear before. He started imagining how the mole must look from close up. Big and brown, like a mud pie. It was probably making Robin sick. He knew he was getting sick just thinking about that mole.

"Okay," a relieved Robin said in his ear.

"What?"

"The song's over."

"Oh." He quickly dropped his hands.

"You don't want to try another one, do you?"

"Was I that bad?" Jonathan asked anxiously.

"No. You were fine."

Jonathan looked at Robin closely. She didn't seem any the worse for wear from her experience. "Then let's dance some more."

Robin looked at Jonathan with surprise. "All right. I thought . . ."

"Thought what?"

Robin rubbed her hands on her jeans. "My hands were perspiring."

"Were they? I didn't notice."

Jonathan supposed he had had a long conversation with his mother on the way home, but he couldn't remember a word of what was said. In his head, he was dancing, not in Robin's bedroom but like that guy in the old movies, Fred Astaire, flying around a huge dance floor, each move executed exquisitely.

Only when they were nearing home did he actually pay attention to something she was saying.

"You know, I taught David to dance," she told him wistfully. "I could have taught you, too."

"I know, Mom." He patted her hand. "But

Robin was more my"— he started to say *style* but thought that might hurt her feelings— "height."

"Oh." Then Mrs. Rossi changed the subject. "I thought you had practice today, Jon."

Jonathan was taken aback. He didn't think his mother would remember that. "Well," he began slowly. "We had a practice yesterday." That wasn't a lie, but it sure was an evasion and he didn't feel good about it.

"So, they canceled today?"

"Uh-huh," Jonathan finally muttered.

Mrs. Rossi took her eyes off the traffic. "You are enjoying basketball, aren't you, Jon?"

Two lies in the space of ten seconds. This was some sort of record for him. "It's okay."

Mrs. Rossi pulled into the driveway. "You don't sound very enthusiastic."

"Things are a little rough right now." He hated having to pick and choose his words this way. "You know we're not doing too well," he said.

"Well, don't let it get to you."

Oh no, Jonathan thought to himself, I wouldn't do that.

As they walked through the garage into the house, Mrs. Rossi said, "I forgot to tell you, there's a letter for you."

"For me?"

"It's from Mark."

Jonathan went to the hall table, where the mail was kept, and ripped open his letter. "Hey, Mom," he called, "Mark wants me to come and visit over Christmas vacation."

His mother stood in the entryway, smiling. "I know. Janice wrote me, too."

"Can I go?" Jonathan asked eagerly.

"Well, we'll have to talk to your father about it. David had a week with Grandpa in New York last summer, so I think it's your turn."

Jonathan whooped with excitement. "Can we talk to Dad tonight?"

"Dad's away on business. Did you forget?"

"Oh, right. We can ask him when he calls, can't we?"

Mrs. Rossi ran her hand through her hair. "I think it's better if I speak with Dad about this first."

Jonathan wanted to know his dad's decision, right now, tonight, but he also knew it was smarter to let his mother handle things. "Okay." He scanned the letter once more. "Mark says he's going to show me Fisherman's Wharf and the zoo." Jonathan looked up at his mother. "And he wants to take me to a concert at the San Francisco Symphony Orchestra."

Mrs. Rossi smiled. Then as she turned back toward the kitchen, Jonathan heard her mutter something. It sounded like "I may leave out the part about the symphony."

C H A P T E R
ELEVEN

"It's got to be today," Bobby Glickman insisted.

A soccer ball rolled away from a fifth-grade pickup game and came at Jonathan, who kicked it away viciously. "Why today? I just missed practice on Friday. I can't miss it again."

"Here's Ham. He'll agree with me."

Ham ambled up to the corner of the school yard where Bobby and Jonathan stood. As soon as he got within earshot, Bobby said, "Will you tell Rossi we have to dig up the magazine today."

Ham's nod was earnest. "Yep. Today."

"But why? We've waited this long."

"That's just it," Ham explained. "We couldn't do it over the weekend because we were all busy. And the weather's been great up until now. But it's supposed to get colder, and even snow. I want to see that magazine a lot, but I don't want to dig through three feet of snow to do it."

"I missed basketball practice on Friday," Jonathan repeated stubbornly.

"Okay," Bobby said. "We'll go without you."

"I don't want you to go without me," Jonathan exploded. "Not after all I went through, almost having a heart attack when Davidson came in . . ."

Ham took a candy bar out of his pocket and unwrapped it. "You've got two choices. You go or you don't go."

Jonathan sighed. He really wanted to go. "All right. I'll think of something to tell Davidson. You know, Ham, I heard of a kid who died from eating Snickers for breakfast." He turned and headed for school.

"Did not," Ham called after him.

"Dead. A peanut got lodged in his wind-pipe."

"Liar," Ham murmured, but he shoved the candy back in his pocket, anyway.

173

All day long Jonathan debated. Was it better just to skip practice or should he go to the coach and make something up? He also wondered whether this qualified as a moral dilemma or just a stupid situation in which he had gotten himself involved. Finally, he decided that he would forget about basketball and head for the empty lot after school. Skipping practice was getting easier and easier to do.

The hallway was filled with kids getting books and coats from their lockers at three o'clock. Jonathan was hoping to make a quick getaway when Robin came up to him as he was throwing his book bag over his shoulder.

"Jon, do you want to come over this afternoon and practice dancing some more?" she asked.

Jonathan felt like slime. Not only would there be no dancing, he'd be in the middle of a vacant lot staring at pictures of ladies' breasts instead. "I can't, Robin," he said, not daring to look at her.

"Well, you're not going to basketball practice. Was it canceled?"

"No, I'm going to the—" he looked around wildly for a cue. A poster decorated with flowers was taped to the window of Mr. Jacobs's room—"flower store."

"The flower store?"

"I mean, the florist."

"Why do you need to go . . ." Then Robin stopped and put her hand over her mouth. "Oh."

Oh? Why was Robin saying "Oh" as if she had just let some tabby out of the bag?

Robin motioned Jonathan closer. "My dress is green," she whispered.

"Green?" Cripes. She thought he was going to the florist to pick out a corsage for the dance.

Jonathan tried to backpedal. "But maybe I shouldn't. I mean, you girls did decide you weren't wearing corsages."

"I wouldn't mind being the only girl who got one," she said boldly.

"Okay then, green. I'll remember that." How had he gotten himself into this mess?

"Hey, Rossi, Ham's waiting outside." Impatience was written all over Bobby's face.

Robin smiled at Bobby. "You mean you're going, too?"

Now it was Bobby's turn to look confused. His eyes darted over to Jonathan, who stood there helplessly. "Yeah, Ham and I are both going."

"Sharon and Jessica are going to be so glad."

"They are?" Bobby was shocked.

Jonathan pulled Bobby away. "See you later, Robin," he called over his shoulder.

Before Bobby could question him, he said, "Don't ask me how I did it, but I just got myself, you, and Ham committed to buying the girls corsages for the dance."

"Smooth move," Bobby said disgustedly.

On the way to the empty lot, Jonathan told them both the whole story. He had to give them credit. They were both laughing by the time they were halfway there.

Ham looked up at the sky. "It looks like it's going to snow."

"It's still too warm to snow," Bobby said.

"Well then, it looks like it's going to . . ." Before he could finish, a drop fell on Ham's nose.

"Oh crud," Jonathan said, "it's raining."

It wasn't a heavy rain, but it was more than a sprinkle. The boys started running to the empty lot, which was only a few blocks away.

"This is it," Ham said as they came to a corner lot full of dead grass. Empty cola and beer cans littered the landscape like little UFOs on the landscape of the moon.

"So where is it?" Bobby shouted above the rising wind.

176

"I buried it under a tree."

There were at least five trees that Jonathan could see. "Which one?"

Ham looked confused. "I think it was the third one from the corner. Or the second one."

Rain whipped through Jonathan's hair. "Why didn't you mark it?"

"Gee, I didn't have any yellow ribbons with me that day," Ham said sarcastically. "Besides, I thought I knew which one it was. But now they all kind of look alike."

"Well let's try the third tree," Jonathan said, pulling his hood up.

They ran over to a large oak tree.

"Where do we dig?" Bobby asked.

Ham bit his lip. "Here." He pointed to a spot beneath the tree. "I think."

"Why don't we each try a side," Jonathan suggested.

"We forgot to bring anything to dig with," Bobby said disgustedly.

"The ground's getting pretty wet. Maybe it will be easy to dig." Jonathan got down on his knees and started turning over earth.

After a few minutes, a shamefaced Ham said, "I think it was that other tree."

Bobby got up and wiped some of the mud

off his pants. The rain was coming down in thick heavy streams now. "Great. That's just great, Ham."

"I'm sure it was that tree," Ham said. He ran over to it and started digging. Bobby and Jonathan began flinging dirt around, too.

"Here it is," Ham said. He tossed over one final scoop of earth and held up the magazine, though it was difficult to tell that's what it was. Sopping wet, the pages were all curled and stuck together. The cover photograph had bled, making the picture almost impossible to see.

The boys huddled together under the tree, although the bare branches didn't offer much protection. Ham peeled several of the pages away from each other and held them up. One seemed to show a woman's body with print all over it. The story from a previous page had stuck to all her interesting parts. Jonathan pulled the magazine away from Ham and rif-fled through the pages, but all the photographs were ruined. Only an advertisement for sunglasses retained its clarity. It was also possible to read an article about how to fix your stereo set.

Bobby rolled up the magazine and hurled it as far as he could throw it. It landed only a few feet away, a testament to Bobby's lack of athletic ability.

"I could have been home watching 'Batman,' " Bobby yelled.

"I should have been in the gym, dribbling," Jonathan added.

Ham looked hapless with water dripping down his nose. "I'm going to catch pneumonia."

Jonathan and Bobby glared at him, but he was so forlorn, Jonathan started laughing. "I wish Veronica Volner could see you now. I'm sure she'd die to go to the dance with you."

Bobby did his best girl imitation, his hand fluttering at his side. "Oh, Ham, I've never seen anyone quite so dashing. I'd go anywhere with you. Just bring an umbrella."

Jonathan laughed until his sides hurt. Even Ham gave in and started laughing, too. They collapsed under the tree. It hardly mattered since they couldn't get much wetter, or dirtier.

Bobby jumped up. "We've got to get out of here or we will catch pneumonia."

"Let's dry off at my house," Ham suggested. "It's the closest."

The boys ran as fast as they could over to Ham's house, where his horrified mother had them change into some old clothes of Ham's.

Then she gave them hot chocolate to warm them up. They spent the rest of the afternoon imagining what they had missed in the magazine and hatching elaborate schemes to procure another one.

By the time Jonathan had to leave, the rain had let up. He cheerfully walked to his house, thinking he couldn't remember when he had had such a good time. He was totally unprepared for the trouble awaiting him.

"Where have you been?" Mr. Rossi walked into the entryway as soon as the door clicked behind Jonathan.

"And what are you wearing?" Mrs. Rossi demanded when Jonathan took off his jacket.

A flannel pajama top and some torn khakis were all Mrs. Berger had been able to find to outfit him. Since Ham was much wider than Jonathan, he looked as though he had gotten lost in the Husky section of the boy's clothing department.

"My clothes got a little mud . . . that is, wet. Mrs. Berger said she'd wash them."

"Mrs. Berger?"

"What were you doing at Ham's when you were supposed to be at practice?" his father demanded.

Jonathan took his time hanging his coat in

the hall closet. "I went over to Ham's after school."

"But you were supposed to be at practice," Mr. Rossi said. "I thought I'd do you a favor and pick you up because of the rain. I felt like an idiot when Coach Davidson said you hadn't been there for two sessions."

Mrs. Rossi held up her hands. "All right, all right. Let's go into the kitchen and discuss this like civilized people."

"After you," Mr. Rossi said grimly, stepping back so Jonathan could lead the way into the kitchen. There was no hope of escape.

"Maybe I should make us all a cup of hot chocolate," Mrs. Rossi said as Jonathan and his father seated themselves on opposite sides of the table.

"No hot chocolate," Mr. Rossi snapped. "Now first of all, where were you last Friday?"

"At Robin's," Jonathan said miserably. "Learning to dance."

"Jonathan, when I picked you up at Robin's, I got the distinct impression your practice had been canceled," Mrs. Rossi said quietly.

"Well, that was sort of the impression I wanted you to have, I guess."

"And what about today?" Mr. Rossi wanted to know.

Jonathan played with the salt shaker. "Today I just felt like goofing around with Ham and Bobby."

"Goofing around?" Mr. Rossi exploded all over again. "How can you expect to play on a team when you prefer goofing around, as you so elegantly put it?"

"I don't know."

Mrs. Rossi started over. "Jonathan, it's not that you can't do other things—"

"What do you mean?" Mr. Rossi broke in. "He can't be running all over this town when he's supposed to be playing basketball."

"Mitch, I just meant, as long as he tells us . . ."

"It isn't a matter of telling us. When you're on a team, you have a commitment to that team. Oh, never mind, you wouldn't understand."

"Because I'm a woman?" Mrs. Rossi asked, her voice rising.

"Well, yes."

"I know what it's like to be on a team," Mrs. Rossi said. "If you remember, I was on my college tennis team."

"Tennis?"

"I'm sorry if that's not macho enough for you."

"Mom, Dad," Jonathan broke in miserably. "I'm sorry. Don't fight."

They both stared at their son. "I guess we are getting a little away from the issue here," Mr. Rossi said gruffly.

Jonathan got up. "Look, I'm sorry. I was wrong. I'll apologize to Coach Davidson, okay? And I won't miss practice anymore."

Mr. Rossi clasped his hands in front of him. "Jon, it's like I told you . . ."

Practice makes perfect. Jonathan silently said the words along with him. Then he ran upstairs.

C H A P T E R
TWELVE

It wasn't easy, but on Wednesday Jonathan made himself go up to Coach Davidson and offer his apologies. "I'm sorry I missed practice," he said, his head down, looking at the scuffed wooden floor.

Coach Davidson stared down at him. "Rossi, I wonder if you want to be on this team."

Suddenly, it was crystal clear to Jonathan. He didn't. He didn't want to practice, he didn't want to play, and he didn't want to miss doing things he enjoyed because of basketball. Those thoughts had been drifting through his mind for a while, like the snowflakes that were lazily falling outside the gym window, but they had never come together like that before. The idea shocked him, and he pushed it away.

"Rossi, I'm asking you something. Do you want to be on the team?"

Jonathan couldn't meet the coach's eyes. "I'm going to keep playing," he mumbled. What else could he do?

"Then no more missed practices or I'll make the decision for you. Hit the court now and get going."

For reasons Jonathan didn't understand, it was his best practice session in a long time. He seemed to have a special connection with Billy, setting up shots for him and passing the ball right into his waiting arms.

Even more surprising, this newfound ability of Jonathan's stuck around for the game with the Blue Point Rams. Not only did the Wildcats win, Jonathan was the second highest scorer, right behind Billy.

He knew he should feel happy, but he didn't really. Instead of making him want to stay on the team, his newfound prowess just seemed like some kind of a cosmic joke.

"See," Billy said as he pulled on his jeans after the game. "I knew you could do it."

Jonathan was tired. "Yeah, it was okay."

Billy frowned. "Okay. That's all it was for you?"

"What do you mean?" Jonathan asked as he buttoned his shirt.

"Hey, I don't know about you, but I get a high off a good game."

Jonathan didn't say anything, but he still felt pretty low.

Mike stepped over to them and clapped Billy on the shoulder. "Great game, Page."

"Thanks."

"That play in the second period was fantastic. You were surrounded. I don't know how you made the shot."

Billy, his face glowing, began reliving the play. Jonathan drifted away. Then he looked back over his shoulder at Mike and Billy, still talking animatedly. All he wanted to do was go home.

"Hey, hero," Mr. Rossi said as Jonathan slid into the front seat next to his father.

"Dad, I'm hardly a hero."

"You looked good out on the court. A few more games like that and Coach Davidson is going to forget he ever heard the name Billy Page."

Jonathan stared out the window into the

inky darkness. So now that he had finally done well in a game, his dad was pleased. Unwillingly, his mind slipped back to his father yelling at him about skipping practice. A few successful baskets sure made a difference.

"Let's stop at The Hut and get a couple of hamburgers," Mr. Rossi said. "And we can discuss Christmas vacation. I know you've been invited to San Francisco, Jon, but I have an idea that might appeal to you more."

Jonathan turned and looked at his mother, who seemed as surprised as he was.

Mr. Rossi put off all Jonathan's questions until after they were settled and he had given the waitress their orders. Then he leaned forward and said. "Jon, I've got some good news."

"What, Dad?"

"You know that client of mine, Ben Simpson? The one who sells sporting goods?"

Jonathan nodded. His dad was always saying Mr. Simpson was going to get them some free gear, but he never did.

"Well, he finally came through for me."

"What are we getting?"

"Better than a free basketball, kiddo. He got us some tickets for the Bears–Vikings game in Minnesota. The seats are on the fifty-yard line.

Simpson's going, too, and can introduce us to some of the players. I thought we could drive up early and make a vacation out of it."

"When's the game?" Jonathan asked warily.

"The second Sunday of your vacation."

Jonathan looked in horror at his mother. That was the day he was supposed to leave for San Francisco.

Mrs. Rossi cleared her throat. "Mitch, that overlaps his trip to California."

"I thought we could all go to San Francisco at spring break. We missed our trip last summer."

Mrs. Rossi looked over at Jonathan, who refused to meet her eyes. "It's not the same. This is the first trip Jonathan would be taking by himself. Why didn't you discuss this with me?"

Mr. Rossi fiddled with his silverware. "I just wanted to surprise you all. When Ben offered me the tickets, it seemed like a great idea." Then he looked at Jonathan's unhappy face. "I guess a trip to San Francisco is a pretty big deal, though."

"Yes it is," Mrs. Rossi said tartly.

Jonathan's throat tightened. Why was he always getting caught in the middle like this?

"Mitch, you can't expect Jonathan to give up this trip."

"No. Of course not. I guess you're getting pretty big, going all that way by yourself," Mr. Rossi said with a small smile.

Jonathan could tell his father's heart wasn't in it, though. "I was looking forward to it," he finally said.

"It's all right, Jonathan. David and I will go. And your mom, too, of course, if she wants."

The waitress came and set down their hamburgers. None of them ate very much.

His mother tried to make him feel better when she came up to say good night. "Don't worry about your father," she said. "He'll get over it."

"I know." He rubbed the edge of his cover. "It just seems like I'm always doing something that gets Dad upset."

Mrs. Rossi sat down on the edge of Jonathan's bed. "Jonathan, in this life you're always going to be upsetting someone. As long as you're not hurting people intentionally, you just have to do what you feel is right."

"But Dad was so excited about going to Minnesota."

"You were excited by Mark's invitation," Mrs. Rossi pointed out.

Jonathan got down farther under the covers. "I'm not that excited about it anymore."

"Think about other things. There's just another week or so of school, and then Christmas vacation. And the next day is the dance."

"Yeah." Even the dance had lost some of its luster.

"Just remember, I'm behind you, Jonathan. And your dad is, too." Mrs. Rossi got up and turned off the light. "Good night, Jon."

Jonathan turned over and then turned over again, trying to find a comfortable spot for himself. So his father was right behind him, huh? Maybe that's why Jonathan was always stepping on his father's toes.

The days before Christmas break were the same as before any vacation. The kids were like penned-up animals waiting to break loose; the teachers tried to pretend that school should carry on as usual, but they couldn't convince themselves of this, much less their students.

There was supposed to be a basketball game before Christmas vacation, but due to an outbreak of chicken pox, the Shipton Pirates had to reschedule. Jonathan tried to look as downcast as the rest of his teammates when Coach Davidson announced the news, but inside he was practically singing: no more basketball, no more practice, no more Davidson. Even if it was only for two weeks, it felt good.

To Jonathan's enormous relief, his father seemed to be accepting his decision to go to San Francisco with good grace. He even joked about it, telling Jonathan not to enjoy the mild California weather too much. "Remember, you've got a whole Chicago winter to get through." Jonathan felt even better when, while they were alone watching television one evening, his father said, "I'm going to miss you when you're gone, Jon."

"You are?"

"Sure I am," Mr. Rossi said, surprised at his son's question. "When you went to overnight camp, I missed you something terrible."

"I didn't know that."

Mr. Rossi lightly touched Jonathan's hair. "I guess I should have told you."

So now the main thing Jonathan had to worry about was the dance—and that stupid corsage.

Ham and Bobby had arranged to meet him at the flower shop on the morning of the dance. None of them wanted the responsibility of buying corsages themselves. They were already waiting in front of Rosie's Posies when Jonathan arrived.

"It's not bad enough that you get us into this," Bobby said, his nose turning red from the cold, "you're late."

"Sorry," Jonathan said curtly.

"Well, let's go in," Ham said.

They all stood there. Finally, Bobby pulled the door open. It made a pleasant little jingle as he walked through, followed by Jonathan and Ham. A round woman with yellow hair piled high on her head was behind the counter arranging delicate white flowers in a vase. A name tag on her smock said Rosie. With surprise, she took in the three glum faces in front of her. "Can I help you?" she asked.

"We need corsages," Jonathan said. "For a dance."

"For our dates," Ham added.

"She didn't think they were for us, dumbo," Bobby said.

Rosie tried to hide a smile. "I'm sure we can find something nice."

"We don't have too much money," Ham warned.

"What is your budget?"

When they gave her the figure each had to spend, she said, "No problem. Let me show you several different things. I'll be right back."

Ham wrinkled his nose. "It smells in here."

"It's a flower shop, Ham," Jonathan said.

Bobby picked up an elegant arrangement with three flowers. "These are nice."

"They're orchids," Rosie said, coming in from the back room. "Very expensive. Let's look at these." The boys huddled around the counters. She held out two delicate flowers. "We could do something nice with carnations, or gardenias. What color are your dates' dresses?"

"My date"—the words felt funny in Jonathan's mouth—"her dress is green."

"White carnations would be nice."

"Fine," Jonathan said, relieved. "White carnations."

"Of course, a pink gardenia would be lovely, too."

Why did she have to go and confuse him? He eyed the flowers as if they were snakes about to bite. "Pink. The pink ones."

"Very good," Rosie said, patting her mountain of hair. "What about you?" she asked, turning to Bobby.

"Her dress is black velvet, so I'm going to go with the white carnations. Black and white is really big," he said confidently.

Jonathan looked at Bobby with admiration. He acted as if he ordered corsages every day.

"An excellent choice." Even Rosie seemed impressed with Bobby's aplomb. She looked over at Ham.

"Do you have any tulips?" Ham asked.

"Tulips?" Jonathan repeated. "Those things that grow in my front yard?"

Rosie was more diplomatic. "It's not the right time of year for tulips. And they usually aren't used in corsages."

"Oh." Ham was disappointed. "I really like tulips. I guess I'll take the white ones, too."

"Now, do you want those to be wrist corsages or the kind with a pin?"

"Wrist," the boys said, practically in unison. There was no way any of them wanted the responsibility of making sure a corsage got pinned in the right place.

The money was doled out and arrangements were made for the flowers to be picked up later. As they left the shop, Ham said, "My dad will pick you up after we get Sharon, okay? About seven."

Jonathan wasn't sure whether that seemed ages away or way too close. He tried to sit down and watch a college football game on television, but when David wandered in, he couldn't tell him the score.

Dinner was a matter of pushing the peas and

lamb chop from one side of his plate to the other. Finally, it was time to get dressed.

"Do you want me to help you?" his mother asked when he pushed himself away from the table.

Even David was disgusted by the question. "Mom, if he's old enough to go to a dance, he can dress himself."

"Well, I didn't mean literally help him," Mrs. Rossi said, offended. "I simply wanted to pick something out for him to wear."

"Annie, Jon's wardrobe isn't so big that he can't find something himself," Mr. Rossi said drily.

"Anyway, I already know what I'm going to wear," Jonathan informed her.

"What?" Mrs. Rossi asked curiously.

"My new pants and a white shirt and the gray sweater."

"Oh, not the gray sweater," Mrs. Rossi cried.

"Why not?"

"It's too small."

"It wasn't too small the last time I wore it," Jonathan argued.

"That was last spring. Your arms are much longer now."

David made like an ape, swinging his arms

and almost knocking them against the dining room table.

"Well, what should I wear?" Jonathan asked, panicked.

Mrs. Rossi got up. "We'll find something."

After a thorough search of his closet, however, even she couldn't come up with anything suitable. "Oh, Jon," she said, sitting down heavily on the bed, "why didn't we think of this before?"

He never thought about what he wore. As far as he was concerned, all apparel was just clothes. Now, suddenly, he was face-to-face with a clothing crisis.

"I know," his mother said, brightening.

"What?"

"You can borrow something from David."

"But he's much bigger than I am."

"Not really. Not anymore."

Despite his worry, Jonathan was glad to hear that he was almost David's size. Maybe he'd be able to beat up on him for a change.

Mrs. Rossi had already walked across the hall and was going through David's closet. She was examining two of David's sweaters when Jonathan walked in, with David right behind him.

"Hey, Mom, those are my best sweaters."

"I know," his mother said absently.

"You're not going to let him wear one, are you?" an outraged David asked.

"Why can't I?" Jonathan demanded.

"You're going to sweat all over it."

"I will not."

Mrs. Rossi raised her voice. "David, I would think you'd be happy to let your brother borrow something for his first dance. And even if he does sweat all over it, as you so delicately put it, we will have it cleaned. As for you, Jonathan, try to be a little more appreciative of David's generosity."

The boys glared at each other, but Jonathan did pick out a blue cable-knit sweater to wear, with David's grudging assent.

"You look wonderful," Mrs. Rossi said, standing at the door as Jonathan got ready to leave.

His father came over to say good-bye. "Have a good time, Jon."

"If you spill one thing on that sweater . . ." David called from the couch.

"I won't, I won't."

"Do you have your corsage?" Mrs. Rossi asked.

"Right here." Jonathan held up the little plastic box of gardenias that was tied with a green ribbon.

"I wish we were driving you," Mrs. Rossi said with a sigh. "I'd love to see how Robin looks. Is her mother taking pictures?"

Jonathan fervently hoped not. But, while Ham and Sharon waited with Mr. Berger in the car, Jonathan was greeted by Mrs. Miller, who held a camera in her hand.

"So nice to see you, Jonathan. Robin will be right down."

Jonathan shook hands with Mr. Miller, hoping his grip was strong, the way his father had taught him it should be. Then he turned and saw Robin enter the living room. She reminded him of Christmas, with her green dress and her red hair framing her face. There was even a sprig of holly in her curls.

Jonathan wanted to tell her how nice she looked, but he didn't know how. Instead, he handed her the flowers and said, "These are for you."

Dumb, dumb, he chastised himself. Who else would they be for?

"Oh, thanks, Jonathan," she said, taking them out of the box. "They're so pretty." She slipped the corsage on her wrist, then a worried look crossed her face. "But my coat will crush the flowers."

"Leave them on for the picture, Robin, then carry them in the box to the dance," her mother said.

Robin looked embarrassed that she hadn't thought of this simple solution.

"All right, let's have a picture now," Mrs. Miller said. She asked Jonathan to take off his coat, and then moved Jon and Robin close together. "Smile now," she said, and then snapped. "How about another one?"

"Mother, people are waiting for us."

"All right. I just hope this one comes out. I'll send your mother a copy, Jon."

"She'll like that." Love it was more like it.

There was a flurry of good-byes and then Jonathan found himself alone with Robin outside. Fortunately, it was just a few steps to the car, and Jonathan didn't have to worry about saying anything. Despite the grief David had given him over the sweater, he silently thanked his brother for his advice about the driving arrangements for the dance. It was worth every bit of the five dollars Jonathan knew he would never see again. Mr. Berger made bad jokes all the way to the community center, embarrassing Ham no end.

The community center gym was usually a pretty bedraggled place, with tired green paint peeling off the walls and a floor that had been scuffed so many times it was tan instead of its original brown. Tonight, however, it had been transformed.

Huge silver snowflakes hung from the ceilings and mounds of white cotton shimmering with glitter bordered the floor. In a corner, a smiling store-window Santa Claus mechanically bowed up and down, a tinny "Ho, Ho, Ho," originating somewhere in the recesses of his huge belly, popped out of his mouth every few minutes.

"Oh, it's wonderful," Robin exclaimed when she entered the gym. "Don't you think so?" she asked.

"Yeah, wonderful."

"Doesn't my corsage look nice?" Robin asked shyly, holding out her hand with the gardenia tightly around her wrist.

"Yeah, it does." Suddenly, it didn't matter that he had bumbled his way into buying Robin flowers. He was just glad he had gotten them for her.

The dance floor was beginning to fill up. A DJ in the corner had put on a fast song, and couples were twisting wildly to the throbbing beat. Jonathan knew he should ask Robin to dance, yet he didn't want to take the first tentative step out to the middle of the floor.

"I guess we should dance," Robin said.

"Right now? Don't you want some punch or something?" He nodded over at the refreshment table, where plates of tiny sandwiches encircled a giant punch bowl.

"Not yet." She walked out to the dance floor, followed by Jonathan.

Despite his misgivings, Jonathan found that once he actually began to put one foot in front of the other, he was dancing. When the first song ended and the second one began, he didn't even hesitate.

"You're really good, Jon," Robin said over the din.

"Practice makes perfect," he responded cheerfully.

Now that he was more comfortable on his feet, Jonathan had time to look around the dance floor. Sharon and Ham were nearby, but Ham's eyes weren't on his partner. Jonathan followed his gaze to Veronica and Billy, swaying together in the middle of the floor. Jonathan hadn't been surprised when he heard that Billy was going to take Veronica to the dance. Those two had seemed destined to find each other. But he was taken aback by Billy's lack of grace on the dance floor. He moved like the Tin Man in *The Wizard of Oz*.

"I'm out of breath," Robin said as the third song started up. "Why don't we have some of that punch now?"

"Sure," Jonathan said cheerfully. Seeing Billy dance had put him in a very good mood.

They wandered over to the refreshment table and each took a cup of punch and a sandwich. They were awfully small, and Jonathan would have liked a couple more, but he didn't want to seem like a pig.

Once they were seated on folding chairs, Jonathan tried to think of something witty to say, but nothing came to mind. It was Robin who began talking as normally as could be, just as though they were sitting in the cafeteria instead of this winter wonderland.

"You and Bobby and I should meet during vacation to exchange books. Miss Morris will probably start the battles right after we get back. Do you have many more to read?"

Jonathan's heart sank. Not many, he thought—only about nine and a half.

"Is something wrong, Jonathan?"

Instead of telling her the status of his reading, he blurted out the question that was never far from his mind. "Robin, what would you think if I quit the basketball team?"

Robin looked at him in amazement. "After what you said to Ham about quitting?"

"I understand Ham a lot better now," Jonathan said miserably.

"But you played well at the last game."

"I know."

"You're getting better."

"Yeah, I just don't like it any better."

Robin played with the band of her corsage. "All I can tell you is what I said to Ham. Nobody can force you to stay on the team. It's your decision to make."

But was it? Jonathan wondered. There were other people who would be affected by what he did: Mike, Billy, the rest of his teammates, but especially his dad. How was he going to keep everyone happy and keep himself happy, too?

C H A P T E R

THIRTEEN

By the time his mother called him for breakfast the next morning, Jonathan was already dressed. He had spent a restless night, with dreams about dancing and basketball interrupting each other.

Telling Robin how he felt about basketball had taken a little of the luster off the evening. They had danced some more and played the games that the community center staff had planned, but, as usual, the Wildcats were ruining things for him. He couldn't get his stupid problem out of his mind, and then he was angry with himself for letting it ruin the dance.

The only thing that banished basketball was

a conversation in the bathroom that had happened near the end of the evening. Jonathan and Bobby were washing their hands when Mike sauntered in.

"So," Mike said with a leer, "it's getting to be that time."

"What time?" Jonathan asked blankly.

"Time to take our dates home, dope."

Bobby caught on right away. "Oh, like you have plans for you and Candy?"

"Sure I do. Her parents are away for the weekend, and her grandmother's staying with her. She'll be asleep when we get home." He smacked his lips together obnoxiously.

As they walked out of the bathroom, Jonathan hesitantly asked Bobby, "What about you and Jessica?"

Bobby shrugged. "I suppose I'll kiss her good night. I'm not planning any big make-out session like Mike. Of course, you can believe about a tenth of what he says, anyway."

As Bobby drifted off to find Jessica, Jonathan waited in the hall, thinking. He saw now that he should have considered this kissing business more carefully. He didn't want to be left out if everyone was going to be kissing their dates good night, but he didn't have a clue as to how one went about it. He searched his pockets for some gum in case he did decide to make a move, but he didn't have any. He vowed never again to be caught at a dance without a pack of gum.

"Jon?" Robin stood in the doorway of the hall. "Bobby said he didn't know what happened to you."

"I was just looking for some gum."

"I have gum in my purse."

Jonathan followed Robin into the gym and pondered the meaning of this. Did that mean Robin was expecting to be kissed? Or did she just like gum?

He worried about whether to kiss or not to kiss for what was left of the dance and all through the ride back to Robin's. When he got out of Mr. Berger's car and walked Robin to the door—as his mother had told him to—he realized that with the porch lights on at the Millers, if a kiss was to take place, it would be in plain sight of Sharon, Mr. Berger, and worst of all, Ham.

"I had a really nice time," Robin said. She seemed a little nervous herself.

"Me, too." It was now or never. Jonathan was about to lean forward when he was interrupted by a short but loud blast from Mr. Berger's horn.

"I guess Ham's dad is in a hurry," Robin said.

"Yeah. Gotta go." He smiled awkwardly and hurried down the steps.

Annoyance mingled with relief, but Jon decided that maybe dances were enough for the sixth grade. He'd try kissing when he got into seventh.

"Jonathan, do you want breakfast or not?" his mother called from the bottom of the stairway. Since she was being so insistent, he expected French toast, or at least an egg. Instead, a box of cereal and a carton of milk sat on the table. His mother was wearing her coat and hat.

"Where are you going?" he asked as he sat down.

"Your dad and I have some errands to run. Christmas is coming," she said with a wink.

"Don't forget that new video game I want."

Mrs. Rossi pulled on her gloves. "Maybe Santa will bring it for you."

"Oh, Mom." Jonathan groaned.

"David's out, but he'll be back soon. I hate to mention this, Jon, but since you're going to be in San Francisco, don't you think it would be a good idea to do some homework?"

"Homework!"

"Well, you have homework, I presume."

He sure did. His composition about a moral dilemma was staring him in the face.

When the house was empty, Jonathan went upstairs and sat at his desk, a blank piece of paper in front of him. He sat there for a long time.

Most of the kids had already chosen what they were going to write about. Bobby's paper was about the time his acting teacher had told him a special audition for a commercial was being held. Since his teacher was going out of town, he asked Bobby to call two other boys and give them the information. Bobby finally did tell them, but he had been sorely tempted not to. Ham's dilemma involved his own bumbling. He had knocked over his mother's best vase and when she asked him what had happened, he had blamed it on his little brother, who at the time was too young to defend himself. Ham had gotten away with the lie, but he had always felt bad about it. It was still a dilemma, because Ham didn't know whether to tell her the truth at this late date. Should he let her know she had a tenacious liar for a son, or keep his secret and feel bad about it for the rest of his life.

Jonathan slumped over his desk, his empty

notebook mocking him. It wasn't that he didn't have a dilemma in mind, it was just that he didn't want to write about it. He didn't even want to think about deciding whether he should quit the basketball team.

Pushing himself away from his desk, Jonathan flung himself down on the bed. He closed his eyes and thought of all the things he would have time for if his time was his own. He could do the reading for the Battle of the Books, listen to music, spend more time with Ham and Bobby just goofing around. He could see Robin.

Then he tried to picture himself giving his father the bad news. There was sound that went along with the picture of his irate father—and it was loud.

"Hey, are you sick?" David stuck his head in the door.

Jonathan rolled over. "Go away, David."

"Oh, I get it, you danced too much." He started whistling "I Could Have Danced All Night."

"Shut up, David," Jonathan yelled.

David put his hands up, "Hey, just kidding, Jon."

"Sorry." Jonathan sat up slowly. "I've just got a lot on my mind."

"Didn't you have a good time last night?" David asked, coming into the room.

"No, it was fine. Really."

"So what's the problem?"

Jonathan hesitated, then he asked, "Did you ever feel like not playing sports?"

David looked bewildered. "No, of course not."

"But there must have been times when you didn't like it," Jonathan probed. "Like earlier in the fall, when your team wasn't playing that well."

"It was hard, but when the going gets tough—"

"Yeah, yeah," Jonathan interrupted him, "I know that's what Dad always says, but how did you really feel?"

"I hated it. The losing, I mean. But I never thought of quitting the team. It never occurred to me."

"Because of Dad?"

David sat down on the edge of Jon's bed. "He was part of it, sure, but mostly I stayed because I wanted to play football."

"You don't like baseball much, and you're going to try out for that in the spring."

David looked down at his hands. "Well, high school baseball might be better than Little League. Like Dad says, I've got to give it a chance."

Jonathan sighed. "Dave, I don't like basketball."

"That's what this is about?" David was shocked. "But you're not thinking about quitting, are you?"

"Yeah, I am," Jonathan admitted.

"Why? Dad says you're improving."

"It's just not what I want to do right now," Jonathan replied simply.

David shook his head. "You'll be making a big mistake. These coaches talk to each other. You'll get a reputation as a quitter. And you know what Dad . . ." David didn't finish his sentence.

Jonathan looked at his brother with pained eyes. "So, you don't think I should do it."

David shook his head slowly. "You'd better think this one over real carefully, Jon."

After David left the room, Jonathan sat lost in thought for a long time. Then he started writing. He didn't stop; he wrote it all in one long burst. When it was done, he read it over.

My moral dilemma is something that's happening to me right now. I'm on the basketball team, but I wish I weren't.

When I first got on the team, I was excited. For one thing I thought I was going to be good at basketball, but that didn't turn out to be the case. I also liked the coach, but then he broke his leg and another coach took over. We spend almost every day practicing and it takes up too much of my time. We also have to do lots of things like push-ups and running laps, which are boring and hard. I just don't like playing basketball.

The reason this is a moral dilemma is because my situation is making me lie. A couple of times I've lied about missing practice. If I keep on playing, I'll probably do the same thing again. I also feel like I'm lying to everyone around me, because I'm staying on the team when I don't want to be there.

You're probably wondering why I don't just quit. There is one person in my family—my dad—who wants me to stay on the team. He thinks I like it, and I don't know how to tell him what I'm really feeling. I know if I quit he'd be hurt, because sports is really important to him, but I don't see how I can stick out the rest of the season, because then I would be lying to myself. So far, I don't know how this dilemma is going to turn out. Somebody is going to be unhappy whatever I do. I'm just not sure who it should be.

When he was finished, Jonathan felt as though he had just done fifty laps and fifty push-ups. He guessed he had completed his homework assignment, but he hadn't solved his problem.

Jonathan wandered downstairs. His parents weren't home yet, and David had disappeared, too. Jonathan was trying to decide whether he should go over to Ham's or Bobby's when the phone rang. It was Robin.

"Hi, Jon. I just called to tell you what a good time I had last night."

Jonathan slid down to the floor, the phone cradled against his ear. "Me, too."

"I was so tired, I didn't get up until ten."

"Me, too."

"Well, I just wanted to say thanks again," Robin said uncertainly.

"Hey, thank you." He cleared his throat. "You looked really nice."

"I did? I mean, thanks." Robin gave a nervous little laugh. "I'd better get off before we thank each other one more time."

After he hung up, Jonathan just stayed on the floor, hugging his knees. He was still there when his parents came through the kitchen door, their arms full of packages.

"What are you doing there?" his father asked with a frown.

"Jon, get up," his mother said, "It's cold down there."

"Right." Jonathan jumped to his feet.

Mr. Rossi put several bags down on the kitchen chair. "You might have to go upstairs for a while." He nodded toward the bags. "We've got to put these in a safe place."

When Jonathan didn't say anything, his father looked at him oddly.

"Did you get any of your homework done?" Mrs. Rossi asked as she set her load down on the kitchen table.

"I finished one assignment."

"Good. Is it anything you want me to go over with you?"

"No." Then Jonathan had an idea. Before he could chicken out, he said, "But I would like Dad to look at it."

"Fine," Mr. Rossi said in a pleased tone of voice. "You almost never let me help you with your homework."

"You're the only one who can help me with this," Jonathan mumbled.

"Let's do it in the den. We can watch the football game while I'm checking it."

Perfect, Jonathan thought, just perfect. It wasn't a long walk to his room, but Jonathan knew how criminals must feel on their way to the electric chair. By the time he picked his composition off his desk, Jonathan was having serious second thoughts about letting his father read it—or turning it in at all, for that matter.

Mustering his courage, he stalked out of the room holding the paper in his hands and went into the den, where the pregame show was blaring from the television set. Silently, he handed it to his father.

Jonathan couldn't bear to observe his father reading his composition, but just leaving the room was impossible. He settled on the couch and began leafing through a magazine, though he saw nothing. He was acutely aware of the moment Mr. Rossi stopped reading and cleared his throat.

"Is this really how you feel about basketball?" he asked in disbelief.

Jonathan nodded mutely and braced himself for what was coming next.

Mr. Rossi merely slumped in his chair, however, and said, "I knew you were frustrated for a while . . ." His words trailed off. Then he asked, "What are you going to do?"

"What do you think I should do?"

Mr. Rossi stayed silent for a long time. "A month ago, I would have forbidden you to quit. But I see you changing every day now, Jon." He shook his head. "I think you know my opinion about playing and doing your best, but you have to make your own choices. And then live with them."

Jonathan leaned forward and tried to explain. "Playing isn't any fun for me, Dad."

"Fun isn't always the most important thing in the world."

"Well, maybe fun isn't what I meant." Jonathan searched for the right words. "Basketball makes me feel like I'm all tied up. My head, my body, my time, too, I guess."

"That's not a good way to feel," Mr. Rossi said.

"No, it stinks," Jonathan murmured.

Mr. Rossi folded and refolded his hands. "It sounds to me as if you've made your decision."

"I guess so." He said it so quietly, he could

hardly hear the words himself. He waited to see what else his father would say, but Mr. Rossi just stared at the television set. Finally, Jonathan got up and walked out of the room. He went to the closet and threw on his coat. Then he went outside.

The air was cold, but it felt good on Jonathan's face. He started walking, even though he wasn't sure where he was headed. When he came to a yard where a man and a little boy were making a snowman, Jonathan stopped and watched for a few seconds. Then he forced himself to move on.

Telling his father he was quitting the basketball team was about the hardest thing he had ever done. And he knew that he hadn't heard the end of it—once his father got over the shock. There was also the matter of letting the coach and his teammates know he was off the team. That wouldn't be easy, either. Right now, though, despite all the sad feeling inside of him, there was also a lightness he hadn't felt in a long time.

A whole vacation stretched in front of him, filled with all kinds of possibilities. After his walk, he would ask his mother to call Aunt Janice to confirm the arrangements for his trip.

Then he would start one of the books on his nightstand that he'd been longing to read. Jonathan stopped his rambling and headed toward home. There were a lot of things he wanted to do.

Emmons Lake
Elementary Library